"Dan will be coming home," Ellen said in a suddenly quivery voice.

"Most likely." Jess didn't say anything else for a long while.

Ellen struggled to absorb the words. How quickly her life had turned upside down. An hour ago...

Her cheeks grew hot. An hour ago she hadn't been thinking about Dan at all. She'd been thinking about Jess Flint.

"Ellen. There's..." he closed his eyes momentarily "...there's more."

Incredulous, she stared at him. "More? What 'more'?" She punched her balled-up fist into his chest.

He caught her hand, imprisoned it in his, and when she tried to jerk out of his grasp, he lifted his arms and pinned her against him. "Ellen. *Ellen.*"

She went perfectly still. "All right, tell me the rest, damn you. Get it over with."

* * *

Loner's Lady
Harlequin® Historical #806—June 2006

Praise for
Lynna Banning

"Do not read Lynna Banning expecting
some trite, clichéd western romance.
This author breathes fresh air into the West."
—*Romantic Reviews Today*

The Scout
"Though a romance through and through,
The Scout is also a story with powerful
undertones of sacrifice and longing."
—*Romantic Times BOOKclub*

The Angel of Devil's Camp
"This sweet charmer of an Americana romance has
just the right amount of humor, poignancy and
a cast of quirky characters."
—*Romantic Times BOOKclub*

The Ranger and the Redhead
"...fast-paced, adventure-filled story..."
—*Romantic Times BOOKclub*

**DON'T MISS THESE OTHER
NOVELS AVAILABLE NOW:**

#803 BROKEN VOWS, MENDED HEARTS
Lyn Stone, Gail Ranstrom and Anne O'Brien

#804 THE CHIVALROUS RAKE
Elizabeth Rolls

#805 THE RANGER
Carol Finch

LYNNA BANNING

LONER'S *Lady*

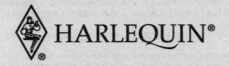

HARLEQUIN®

TORONTO • NEW YORK • LONDON
AMSTERDAM • PARIS • SYDNEY • HAMBURG
STOCKHOLM • ATHENS • TOKYO • MILAN • MADRID
PRAGUE • WARSAW • BUDAPEST • AUCKLAND

ISBN 0-373-29406-9

LONER'S LADY

This edition published by arrangement with Harlequin Books S.A.

® and TM are trademarks of the publisher. Trademarks indicated with
® are registered in the United States Patent and Trademark Office, the
Canadian Trade Marks Office and in other countries.

www.eHarlequin.com

Printed in U.S.A.

Please address questions and book requests to:
Harlequin Reader Service
U.S.: 3010 Walden Ave., P.O. Box 1325, Buffalo, NY 14269
Canadian: P.O. Box 609, Fort Erie, Ont. L2A 5X3

Chapter One

She saw him coming up Creek Road and for a moment her heart stopped beating. Clutching the pitted garden trowel in one hand, she tucked a wayward strand of hair back under her blue sunbonnet and squinted into the late afternoon sun until her vision blurred.

But it wasn't Dan. She released the breath she'd been holding and studied the man. A worn-looking leather saddle weighed down one shoulder, and a dark hat slanted over his eyes. He walked with a slight hesitation in his gait, as if one knee was stiff. Just another saddle tramp looking for a meal.

Ellen watched for a minute, then bent to the row of leafy vegetables and pulled up an extra half-dozen carrots for supper. She couldn't bear the thought of someone, even a saddle tramp, going hungry.

Drawing in a slow lungful of the hot, earth-scented summer air, she resumed weeding. Probably lost his horse in a poker game. She sniffed at the thought and yanked a clump of chickweed out of the ground. What was it about gambling that men found so irresistible?

Getting something for nothing, Dan had told her once with a cocky grin. Ellen knew better. Most often he started with Something and ended up with Nothing.

Pulling the kitchen knife from her apron pocket, she sliced off a dozen yellow squash and two shiny green peppers. At least her simple meal would be colorful.

She straightened again as the man turned in at her gate. It took him a long time to push open the rickety contraption she had cobbled together out of used nails and crooked sugar pine limbs. It sagged badly, the rusted hinge held in place by a single screw. Another of the thousand and one things she hadn't had time to fix.

"Miz O'Brian?"

Ellen stepped out of the vegetable patch toward him. "Yes? I am Mrs. O'Brian."

Jess dropped the saddle where he stood. "My name's Jason Flint, ma'am." From beneath the brim of his hat he studied her face for a flicker of recognition. Nothing. Under her own floppy gingham bonnet, the woman's blue eyes drilled into him like two steel bolts.

"Most folks call me Jess." Again he waited for a reaction, but her sun-reddened features betrayed not a hint of feeling. *Damn and then some. How lucky could he get?*

She stuck out a dirt-stained hand. "Mr. Flint." She had a strong handshake for a small woman, but quicker than he could wink she tucked her hand back into her apron pocket.

"Guess you'd like to know what I'm doing out here on your farm?"

Those blue eyes widened slightly, but she kept her face impassive. She'd make a good poker player, Jess thought. Or maybe she was just a careful farm wife who'd seen a good number of strays in her time.

"Truth is…" he began.

"You're hungry," she stated.

"Yes, ma'am."

Her hands went to her hips. "And broke."

Jess hesitated. "Well…" He'd sold his horse and most of his possessions three days ago so he could eat. Hell yes, he was broke.

"Out-of-work-down-on-your-luck-and-lost-your-horse," she said. It wasn't a question. She ran the words together as if she was reciting a poem.

"Yes, ma'am." He expected her to frown or purse her lips and *tsk-tsk* at him, but she did neither. Instead, she gave him a long look and headed for the back porch of the farmhouse.

Jess let his gaze follow her, hoping she'd say something with the word *supper* in it. He noted the peeling white paint on the house and the lopsided angle of the screen door. A hole as big as his fist gaped in the mesh. He'd bet she had a kitchen full of fat black flies.

The back door wheezed open and slapped shut and her voice floated to him through the screen. "Supper's in half an hour. Wash up at the pump."

Jess swiped off his hat, bent over the pump and splashed cool water on his face, then smoothed a handful of water through his hair. Glancing at the back door to make sure she wasn't watching, he stripped off his shirt and rubbed water over his chest and neck.

Using his shirt, he dried off and shrugged the damp linen back on. The wrinkled garment smelled sweaty as a lathered horse, but at the moment it was the only shirt he owned.

With time to spare before supper, Jess carted his saddle out to the barn, then made a slow circuit of the farmhouse. The weathered paint on the north side looked more gray than white, but crisp white curtains hung at the parlor windows. A single wicker rocking chair sat on the wide front porch.

When he reached the back of the house, the screen door scraped open and he heard her voice again. "Suppertime!" Jess clomped up the back steps, hoping she wouldn't hear his stomach growling.

The first thing he smelled was fresh coffee. The second was hot biscuits, and beyond that he didn't care. This was as close to heaven as he was going to get for a while.

She'd set two places at the battered kitchen table. Painted a fiery red, the finish looked speckled where the original green showed through. Years of hard use had dulled the finish on the white china plates; the only piece that wasn't cracked was the cream pitcher.

She gestured for him to sit, then turned to the stove and scooped fluffy-looking biscuits into a basket. Jess used the opportunity to take a closer look at her.

Not bad. Maybe twenty-five or -six. Trim waist, nicely rounded backside. Suntanned arms, and long, long legs, judging from the length of her blue work skirt. A ribbon tied at the back of her neck kept a tumble of brown curls in check.

Her shirt—a man's work shirt, he noticed—looked mighty incongruous under the ruffled apron.

She turned toward him. "Coffee?"

"Sure. Straight."

Her gaze narrowed. "'Straight' applies to whiskey."

"I meant no cream," he said.

When she spun back to the stove, he glanced at her shoes. Work boots. He should have guessed. She farmed the place by herself. That would explain the dilapidated state of the barn and the henhouse, the peeling paint, the worn planks in the kitchen floor.

She sure didn't talk much. He wondered how long she'd been without a man.

She dished up a platter of sweet corn and a bowl of carrots and squash with something green mixed in. No meat, but he wasn't complaining. She untied her apron, hung it on a nail by the back door and set the basket of biscuits on the table.

Jess waited. After an awkward pause, she passed him the platter of corn. "What are you waiting for? I thought you'd be hungry."

"I am hungry. Just wanted to see if you were the type that said grace."

"Grace!" She snapped out the word like a pistol shot. "The good Lord had little enough to do with putting food on this table."

Jess said nothing. Guess he'd hit a nerve.

Her shoulders relaxed. "I apologize, Mr. Flint. Sometimes it seems like the Lord doesn't even notice how hard I'm working down here."

"You run this place on your own?" He knew the answer, but he wanted to ask anyway.

"Yes." With jerky movements she split open a biscuit and dunked half into the soggy vegetables on her plate.

"How long?"

"Two years and eight months." The sharp edge in her tone said it all. He wondered how she felt about that two years. How much she knew.

"Husband dead?"

Ellen watched him down a gulp of water from the glass at his elbow, and laid her fork beside the plate. "I don't know. He went off to town one day and never came back."

"Gambling man?"

"Yes. No use varnishing the truth."

Her guest looked up. "Mind telling me his name?"

"Daniel. Daniel Reardon O'Brian."

An odd expression crossed the man's sun-darkened face. "Irish, I'd guess," he said in a quiet voice.

She nodded. "The worst part is…" She didn't let herself finish the thought.

Mr. Flint slathered butter onto an ear of pale gold corn. "Got a hired man to help out?"

She leveled a long look at him. "I had one until four months ago. He came back from town smelling of spirits and tried to— No, I don't have a hired man." She leaned forward and skewered him with those eyes again. "And no, I do not want one."

He bit into the corn and chewed in silence.

"It's only a small farm," she explained. "I can keep up the housework and the garden. Planting corn and potatoes and alfalfa keeps me pretty busy. And of course there's the stock."

"Stock?"

"My milk cow, Florence. And the chickens. And one horse."

His eyes flicked to hers and immediately dropped to the biscuit on his plate. "What kind of horse?"

Ellen sniffed. "He's not worth stealing, Mr. Flint. He's a plow horse."

"Wasn't thinking of stealing it, ma'am. I was thinking of riding it."

"Where on earth to?"

"Town. And back."

Ellen regarded him with as much calm as she could muster. He had longish black hair and skin so sundarkened he could be Indian. After a good minute she trusted herself to speak in a civil tone. "For a poker game? For loose women and liquor? For—?"

"For supplies." He growled the words without looking at her.

"Whose supplies?" she snapped. Why were her nerves on edge around this man? She'd fed plenty of wandering cowboys; not one of them had ever riled her like this.

"Yours. How do you tote things from town?"

"I walk. And once a week Mr. Svensen drives a wagon out from the mercantile to collect my butter and eggs. He brings the flour and molasses and other heavy items."

"You don't have a wagon?"

"No, I don't have a wagon. Dan took it." Ellen pressed her mouth into an unsmiling line. He'd taken a few other things as well. Her faith in the silky-voiced Irishman with the dancing eyes. Her trust. Her hope for a child.

Again that puzzling expression came over Mr. Flint's face. Part disbelief, part…anger? She guessed he didn't believe her.

"Surely you don't think I would lie about such a thing?"

"No, ma'am."

Jess wished she had, though. He didn't want to think about the fix husband Dan had left her in. He needed to think about how he was going to do what he'd come here for.

They ate their supper in silence except for the faint burble of coffee on the stove. All at once she seemed to hear it, and flew across the room to shove the blue speckleware pot to one side. "I've overboiled it again! It must taste pretty awful."

"I've had worse. I've made worse myself."

Ellen sighed. "I guess overboiled coffee isn't that important. Farm life has a way of paring things down to essentials. Survival is what's important."

"Yes, ma'am. It surely is. Makes a person wonder just how far they'll go with survival in mind."

He gave her a long look. His eyes were a dark, dark blue, almost black, and the way he scrutinized her started uneasy flutters in her stomach. This man didn't miss much. Did he see how weary she was? How her back ached and her heart was shriveling up? She knew being a good wife meant sticking it out, for better or worse, but oh, how she smarted under the load.

Still, smart she must. No respectable woman on the western frontier caved in to exhaustion or loneliness.

He gave her a lopsided smile and dropped his gaze to his coffee cup, still two-thirds full.

"Miz O'Brian, would you mind if I slept in your barn tonight?" He sent her another crooked smile. A bigger one. The corners of his dark eyes crinkled and a dimple appeared on one sun-bronzed cheek.

Ellen studied him. She'd let the odd cowboy throw down a bedroll in the hay, but not often. Being alone out here three miles from town made her cautious. Mr. Flint made her more than cautious. He asked too many questions, and more than once she'd caught him looking at her as if trying to guess how much she weighed. She felt off balance. Vulnerable.

"Miz O'Brian?"

"I am considering it." His eyes were hungry. Calculating. They made her unsure of things she'd never questioned before. Like why she kept on struggling to keep up the farm, waiting, always waiting, for Dan to return.

Still, she had no cause to be afraid. She kept Dan's loaded shotgun under the sink. "Very well, Mr. Flint. You may sleep in the barn."

"Much obliged, ma'am. I'll feed your stock before I turn in."

"There is no need. Florence needs to be milked, and I—"

"I'll see to it." He took a final swallow of coffee and pushed away from the table. "Thanks for the supper."

He ambled toward the back door, the hitch in his gait even more obvious. Even with the limp, though, she liked the way he moved, unhurried and oddly graceful for a tall man with a stiff knee.

The screen whapped shut behind him. She listened to the uneven rhythm of his boots on the porch steps, then gathered up the two dirty plates and the empty corn platter. She'd cooked a dozen ears; only two cobs rested on her plate. The other ten, chewed clean, were piled high on his plate. The man was more than just hungry; he was starving.

Before she finished drying the dishes, a full metal pail of foamy milk sat inside the back door. Beside it lay a dozen eggs wrapped in a red bandanna. He must have searched under every hen she owned to come up with that many at an evening gather.

Ellen smiled wryly. No doubt Mr. Flint was hinting at breakfast. She scrubbed the last kettle and hung the sodden towel on the rack near the stove. Well, it wouldn't hurt to let him sleep in the barn for one night.

She poured the fresh milk into four shallow milk pans, unloaded the eggs into a bowl and set it all in the cooler off the back porch. By morning there would be more cream, enough to churn and some for scrambled eggs.

That is, if she let him to stay for breakfast. Something about Mr. Flint made her nervous. Maybe it was his eyes. They were the darkest blue she had ever seen, darker even than the morning glories she'd planted along the front fence.

She tried not to think about him as she washed out the milk pail and lifted the lantern from the counter. Halfway up the stairs to her bed, she jolted to a stop. She hadn't even offered him a candle to light his way around the barn.

Maybe he didn't need it. With those predatory eyes he could probably see in the dark.

A shiver crawled up her backbone as she opened the door to her bedroom. Lamplight made the blue patchwork quilt, and the puffy matching pillow covers she'd sewn, glow with inviting warmth. She moved to pull the curtains shut and caught her breath.

Was he watching her window from the barn? Quickly she blew out the lantern flame.

The sooner he was gone, the better. She didn't want to look into eyes that hungry any longer than she had to.

Chapter Two

The rooster woke her. With a groan Ellen planted her bare feet on the floor and forced herself upright. Peach-gold sunlight spread through the cozy room, glinting in the framed mirror on the chiffonier and washing over her needlework basket and the ticking clock on the night table. This morning the light looked soft and creamy as buttermilk.

She washed, then hastily caught her unruly curls with a strip of calico at the back of her neck. On impulse, she leaned forward to inspect her face in the mirror.

Merciful heavens, what a sight! She looked every bit as tired as she felt, even more than the last time she'd looked, which was…let's see…Easter Sunday? Her skin was sun-browned and freckles were sprinkled across her nose. The area around her mouth looked pinched, and her eyes…

Her eyes looked weary, as if ten years of trouble had been added to her life. Worse, there was a hopeless expression in their depths she didn't like one bit. She looked like Mama had before she died. Worn-out. Was this what he saw?

Didn't much matter, she guessed. A woman alone as much as she was got used to the darker side of things.

While she dressed in her blue work skirt and a clean blue shirt of Dan's, she thought about the stranger sleeping in her barn. For no reason she could name, she didn't trust the man.

Come now, Ellen. You must not judge a person by his appearance alone. Even a man with eyes she couldn't read and a way of moving that reminded her of a cat. A big cat, with slim hips and a quiet way of speaking. He set all her nerves on edge.

With a sniff and a quick shake of her head, she marched down the stairs to the kitchen. Nerves or no nerves, she had a farm to run.

Another half bucket of milk sat just inside the back door. Blast the man. All right, she'd fix his breakfast. But first she had to sprinkle some mash for the chickens and turn the cow into the pasture.

She took two steps into the chicken yard and halted. The hens were clucking contentedly over fresh mash already spread in the wooden feeder. Well, of all the...

Ellen headed for the barn.

Florence was not in her stall. And the horse was gone! "Tiny? Where are you, boy?"

She searched the barn, then the yard. If he'd gotten into her carrots again she would scream.

Not in the garden. Not nibbling on green apples in the orchard. Not anywhere she could see.

Damn! That man had stolen her horse!

Oh, how *could* he? After a summer so scorching she'd watered her vegetables with bathwater and sprinkled down the henhouse at night, losing her horse was the last straw. *Why* could she not have one single day without feeling as if all the sand inside her was dribbling out?

Unaccountably, she started to cry. Stinging tears slid down past her nose and dripped onto her shirt front. *Let me have just one day, Lord, when nothing bad happens. When I think I can make it through this.*

No wonder she had aged a decade since Easter.

An insidious question needled into her mind. *Was it worth it to hold on?*

The answer came almost instantly. It *was* worth it. This farm was the only piece of ground that had ever belonged to her, and she'd be damned if she'd give it up. She held on to it partly for Dan, but mostly for herself. She'd scratched a vegetable garden out of a patch of bare earth, planted honeysuckle to spread over the privy, roses and black-eyed Susans and...

Yes, she worked hard to make ends meet, but she loved the place. She couldn't imagine living anywhere else.

Besides, she had nowhere else to go.

Sniffing back tears, she marched out the barn door and slammed it shut, wondered why she'd let that drifter stay.

Because you are lonely. Because she wanted to hear the sound of another person's voice. She wrapped her arms over her belly and shut her eyes. She hurt so much she didn't realize how furious she was until she began to tremble.

Oh, for Lord's sake, pull yourself together.

She snapped open her eyes. Just as she took a step toward the house, something moved in the alfalfa field beyond the creek.

Florence! Thank God. At least he'd left her the cow. Brushing the tears off her face with her shirtsleeve, she gathered up her skirt in one hand and began to run toward the animal.

Her breath hitched, and when she reached the creek bank, she felt a bit dizzy. No time to remove her boots. Instead, she hiked her skirt higher and splashed into the burbling water.

The thin, sharp-faced man behind the counter sent Jess a look of disbelief. "You say Miz O'Brian sent you?"

Jess tightened his lips. "No, I didn't. I said I'd come for her supplies. She didn't send me."

"Fine distinction, mister," the mercantile owner said. "We kinda look out for the lady, see. Ever since her husband run off. No one's ever bought supplies for her before."

Jess shifted his weight to his good leg. "I didn't say I was *buying* the goods, just delivering them."

"With what?" Gabriel Svensen had sold sundries in Willow Flat for thirty-five years; no one had ever gulled him out of so much as a stick of peppermint candy.

"I've got a horse outside."

"Yeah, I recognize Tiny all right. You ain't never gettin' a barrel of molasses on that snake-blooded old nag."

Jess bit his tongue. Most times he didn't have to ask for anything twice. But that was back when he was well known. Those days were long gone. "Don't want molasses. What I—Miz O'Brian—needs is a sack of sugar."

"White or brown?" the proprietor snapped.

"White."

Svensen's gray eyebrows shot up, but he said nothing, and Jess pivoted to survey the bushel baskets of produce arranged at the front of the store. "And a dozen lemons," he added. "And six oranges. She's got credit here, doesn't she?"

Svensen opened his angular jaw with a crack. "She does. You don't. And Miss Ellen's not one to add the fancy things onto her bill. You sure she wants white sugar? And oranges?"

Jess grinned in spite of himself. "I'm sure. She…needs them."

"Hell, maybe she's makin' a batch of marmalade, or a cake, like every other woman in town. What do I know? I'll just wrap 'em up if you'd care to look around."

"I'll wait. It smells good in here."

Svensen spread a length of brown wrapping paper on the counter and went to work. "Reckon that good smell's coming from Iona Everett's bunches of lavender hangin' there on the beam." The shopkeeper tipped his chin up to the timbered roof. "And the shipment of spices and brown sugar that came in yesterday. The ladies are havin' a big cake-baking hoo-rah on Sunday, raisin' money for the new church."

As he talked, he rolled up each orange in a square of paper—"special for Miss Ellen"—laid them on top of the ten-pound bag of sugar and corralled the lemons into a paper sack. Then he bundled all the items up in one neat package and tied it with grocery twine.

"Remind Miz O'Brian about the cake do, will ya? She deserves an afternoon off."

Jess nodded. "She does." He scooped up his package and had turned to go when he heard Svensen's raspy voice.

"You watch your step around Miss Ellen, mister. She's a real lady, even if she does work a farm."

Jess nodded again and strode outside to the hitching rail where he'd left the horse. Tiny, was it? He chuckled. The only "tiny" things were the *other* horses tied at the rail. The huge head of the plow horse towered over all of them.

He plopped the bulky package on Tiny's sturdy back and heaved himself up. The horse was so broad his saddle wouldn't fit; he'd left it in the hayloft with his saddlebag, and ridden bareback. Clicking his tongue, he walked the animal down the main street and onto Creek Road.

Ellen. So her name was Ellen. He wondered how long it would take before she let him call her that. She didn't know it yet, but he planned to stay. For as long as it took.

He reined up at the sagging front gate and slipped off the horse to wrestle it open. It needed another screw and ten minutes of his time. He'd do it after breakfast.

His stomach gurgled as he led Tiny through the gate and maneuvered the rickety thing closed. Maybe another hinge, as well. And some real wood, not these curlicue pine branches she'd used.

At the back porch steps he halted and peered through the screen door. "Miz O'Brian?"

The kitchen was empty. He scanned the garden and the spindly looking apple trees at the back fence. Where the hell was she?

He tramped into the house, checked the neat parlor, where crocheted doilies lay on the arms of the faded green velvet settee, then climbed the stairs and checked each of the four bedrooms. All empty. Maybe the barn?

By the time he'd rubbed Tiny down with an old gunnysack and given him some oats, there was still no sign of Ellen. An odd prickle swept up the back of Jess's neck. He headed for the henhouse, but found nothing but clucking brown chickens and one lordly rooster. Maybe she was visiting a neigh—

He heard something. He shushed the chickens and listened.

A voice. Thin-sounding and some distance away, but calling out at regular intervals.

"Miz O'Brian?" Jess shouted. He took a step toward the sound. "Ellen?"

Another faint cry, and Jess headed toward the creek. What was she doing down there? "Ellen? Miz O'Brian?"

A weak cry carried to him and his breath stopped. She was hurt. A cold sweat started at his hairline. Oh, God, no. *What had they done to her?*

Without thinking he began to run.

Chapter Three

She lay in the creek bed, the lower part of her body half in the water, her skirt rucked up to her knees. Her head rested on a lichen-covered stone, and he could see one leg was folded under her at an odd angle. Jess stumbled down the bank and splashed across to her, a rock lodged in his gut.

She looked up at him with weary eyes. "What are you doing here?"

Jess knelt beside her, his heart hammering. "A better question might be what are *you* doing here?"

She tried to smile. "Chasing the c-cow into the pasture, and I s-slipped on a rock." Her voice sounded close to breaking. Her body shivered violently, and Jess reached to touch her arm. Her skin was like new snow.

"How long have you been here?"

Her eyelids fluttered closed. "Since dawn. I got up to milk…" Her voice trailed into silence.

"I milked earlier," Jess said.

"Tiny was gone, and... Anyway, the cow..."

Jess leaned over her. "Don't talk, Ellen. Save your strength. I've got to get you out of the creek, and it isn't going to be easy."

"Hurts when I move," she murmured.

"Got any laudanum up at the house?"

She shook her head.

"Whiskey?"

"Just some wine. Port. In a decanter on the top shelf. It was a..." she gave a soft laugh "...wedding gift."

"I'll get it."

He started to stand up, but her fingers grabbed at his arm. "No. Don't leave. Please don't. I will manage without it."

Jess studied the position of her body. Looked like a broken tibia. Should he straighten her leg first? Or lift her up and let the injured limb right itself? Either way it would hurt like hell. Maybe he could pull her backward up the creek bank, see if her leg would straighten naturally.

He straddled her, one knee in the cold creek water, the other on the bank, and dug his hands into the mud beneath her armpits. As gently as he could, he hoisted her farther up the slope. Her face went white as parchment. Her breathing hitched and she balled her hands into fists, but she didn't make a sound.

Dragging her was no good, he realized. Too painful and too slow. He needed to get her to the house, and fast.

"I'm going to be sick," she moaned. Clamping her palm over her mouth, she stared up into his face, a desperate, trapped look in her eyes.

"It's okay, Ellen. Listen to me. I'm going to lift you up. It's going to hurt, but it's the only way."

She nodded once.

"Put your arms around my neck and hold on," he ordered.

When her cold, shaking hands met at his nape, Jess carefully scrabbled away the wet earth under her shivering form until he could slide one hand under her shoulders. Gritting his teeth, he bent and slipped his other hand under her knees.

When he lifted her from the muddy bank, she released a strangled cry, but he stood up slowly, cradling her body in his arms. Her injured leg unfolded and she cried out again.

A choking sensation closed his throat. Trying not to jostle her any more than necessary, Jess picked his way up the slippery incline, concentrating on her jerky breathing rather than the ache in his own leg. When he reached level ground, he started toward the house. It seemed a hundred miles away.

He stepped every inch of the way with her moans of agony in his ear, his nerves twisting at every inarticulate sound she made. Jess unclamped his jaw. "You all right?"

"Of course I'm not all right," she muttered through clenched teeth.

He kept moving. Halfway across the yard, she tugged on his shirt, and he heard her whisper, "Talk to me."

"I can't think of a damn thing to say," he admitted.

"Talk to me anyway."

His mind went blank. What could he talk about? He

hadn't had a woman in his arms since… He didn't want to think about it.

After a long minute, he began to sing in a low, scratchy voice. "'Whippoorwill singin', and the owl's asleep. I'm beggin' you, Lord, my soul to keep.'"

Ellen pressed her ear closer to his chest. Underneath the smell of damp mud, he caught the faint scent of roses from her hair. "More," she murmured.

"That's all there is. Kind of a one-verse song."

"Either you sing," she said in a tight voice, "or I'll start screaming."

Jess sucked in a long breath. "That might be better than my singing."

"Not for me," she snapped.

It sounded as if her jaw was clenched. "Sorry. I wasn't thinking."

"Don't think, Mr. Flint. Sing."

"Yes, ma'am. All right, here goes. 'Tater has no eyes to see, sweet corn cannot hear. Beans don't snap, date palms don't clap, that's why I like my beer!'"

What a choice. He was drunk when he'd made it up, and drunk when he sang it. He sure as hell wasn't drunk now.

He reached the back porch steps, angled sideways and yanked the screen door open. It fell to one side with a clatter. He'd repair it after breakfast, he thought. With Ellen down, there would be more to do than fix screens and gates.

In spite of himself, he smiled. Now she'd be forced to have him stay on as a hired man. Things couldn't have worked out better if he'd planned it.

* * *

Upstairs in the blue-papered bedroom, Jess stooped to lay her on the bed, but she stopped him with a sharp "No!"

"What do you mean, no? I've got to take a look at your leg. Might have to splint it. You'd best be lying flat."

"My skirt is muddy." She gestured with her hand. "My grandmother's quilt…"

Without a word Jess dipped toward the bed and pulled the pretty blue quilt onto the floor. It smelled faintly spicy. The whole room did, he noted. Maybe a bunch of Iona Everett's lavender…

He laid Ellen down on top of the sheet. After breakfast, there'd be a washing to do, as well.

Ellen gritted her teeth. God, oh God, it hurt! She couldn't feel her toes, but somewhere between her thigh and her ankle, a saw was slicing into the bone. "Get the port," she managed to gasp.

She heard his boots clump down the stairs, then back up. In his hands he held the decanter of purple-brown liquid and a water glass. She shut her eyes against the nausea sweeping over her, listened to the clink of the decanter neck on the edge of the tumbler, and the gurgle of the wine as it sloshed out. She could tell by the sound that he filled the glass to the top. She could hardly wait to swallow a big mouthful.

He steadied her hand around the glass and lifted her head off the pillow so she could drink. "Wonderful," she breathed as the warmth of the first gulp spread down into her belly. "Tastes like melted raisins."

"Drink some more. Then I'm going to look at your leg."

"I don't want to move, so can you leave my skirt on? Just pull it up?"

Jess hid a smile. It wasn't the first time he'd tossed up a woman's skirts. But this time sure felt less arousing.

"Ready?"

She downed another mouthful and nodded.

He unlaced her wet boots and drew them off, trying not to listen to her gasps of pain. Raising the sodden hem of her skirt and the petticoat underneath, he gently lifted the fabric up to her waist. At the first sight of her drawer-covered limb he knew what had happened. The front leg bone had snapped just below the crest.

From her undergarments rose the smell of soap and something spicy. Too bad he'd have to cut that lacy material away. He pulled the ruffled cotton petticoat to discreetly cover her bare knees. He might have traveled on the shady side of the law, but he was still a gentleman.

"Your right leg is broken," he said carefully. "You've got two choices, Miz O'Brian. I can take Tiny and ride for a doctor, or I can set the bone myself."

She groaned. "Dr. Callahan—he's my uncle—lives in town. Too far."

Jess bit his lower lip. "How close is your nearest neighbor?"

"Gundersen place," she whispered. "Seven miles."

Oh, God. He would have to do it.

In the kitchen he boiled a kettle of water, tore a clean dish towel into strips and searched for a knife. The worst part for him would be cutting her drawers off. The worst part for her would be when he explored the break.

He stuffed a sharp paring knife under his belt and turned to the back door. Outside, he strode to the front gate and snapped off two relatively straight branches to use as a splint. On his way back through the kitchen, he lifted the kettle off the stove and grabbed a china bowl from the dish shelf.

Upstairs the sun threw dappled light across the upper part of her body. She rested the wineglass on her chest, holding it with both hands. Almost empty, he noted. Good girl.

Grasping the knife, he bent and started slicing at the lacy hem of her drawers. He slit them halfway to her waist, and she didn't make a sound until he straightened.

"How does it look?"

"Your left leg is fine." It was the right leg that made his breath catch. Under the pale skin he could see the bulge of the bone where it had separated. "To set the break in your right leg properly, I'll have to manipulate it."

Jess wiped his fingers across his forehead; they came away wet with sweat, which didn't surprise him. He'd rather rob the Ohio Central than put his hand on her leg.

"Don't drag it out," she muttered from the bed. "Just get it over with."

"Don't rush me," he countered. "I like to take my time with some things."

He was damn glad she didn't ask *what* things. He settled one hand on her knee, then cupped the joint with his other. Watching her face, he moved both hands toward the break. The closer he got, the tighter she scrunched her eyes shut.

His belly knotted. "I'm sorry, Ellen." Gently he eased

his fingers onto the bulge of skin, then felt below her knee with his other hand. There it was, plain as pudding. He could feel how the edges of the bone fit together.

Mentally he reviewed exactly what he had to do. Before he made a move, he glanced up at her face. Hell, she was sweating worse than he was. He'd try to make it quick.

He braced himself. Holding one hand steady under the break, he pressed his palm down hard from the top. Her anguished scream sent a sharp, cold blade into his chest, but an instant later he heard the soft snap as the bone shifted back into place.

She screamed again.

"Yell if you want, just don't move," he ordered.

While she panted on the bed, he laid out the make-shift splints. One of the gate sticks curved just the right way along her leg; the other was straighter, but it would do. He bound them in place with strips of toweling.

"Better," Ellen murmured. Her leg ached like a plow had hooked into it, but it wasn't the searing pain she'd endured earlier. "How did you learn to do that?"

"Spent some time as an army surgeon during the war."

Thank the Lord. She wouldn't ask which army. Reb or Federal, she was grateful for the man's skill.

He straightened suddenly, reached for the decanter of port and tipped it into his mouth.

"I'd offer you my glass," she said, "but...oh, here." She thrust the tumbler at him anyway. "You've earned it."

He smiled for the first time in what seemed like hours. He'd shaved since supper last night, she noticed. The dimple in his cheek reappeared.

She watched him pour hot water from the kettle into

her best vegetable bowl and drop in a piece of toweling. Clean, she hoped.

He bent to smooth the wet cloth over her good leg, washing off the streaks of dried mud with a surprisingly light touch. "I don't fancy cutting you out of your skirt and petticoat. Seems like a waste of serviceable garments. Got any ideas?"

What an incredible topic of conversation! Still, it had been an unusual day, and it was still only ten o'clock, she judged, glancing at the sun outside the window.

"If you could undo the fastenings at my waist, you could just pull my skirt and petticoat off over my head."

"Yeah, I thought of that." Taking it slow and easy, he washed her broken limb from the ankle to the break, then started at her upper thigh and worked down as far as her knee. When he finished, he set the bowl of grimy water on the floor and leaned over her.

"The skirt button's at the back," she said. "Petticoat has a ribbon tie."

"Usually does," he answered.

Ellen's eyebrows lifted. She felt his hands reach under her waist, fumble the skirt button through the buttonhole and then untie the ribbon of her petticoat.

He moved to the head of her bed. "Arms up," he ordered.

Ellen obliged, grateful that she didn't need to move her throbbing leg to rid herself of her clothes. She felt both garments slide upward, and with her arms raised she managed to shimmy free of them. He tossed them on the floor with the washcloth and caught her gaze. "You want to remove your—"

"Just my shirt," she said quickly. "I'll keep on my camisole and my drawers, what's left of them."

She unbuttoned the blue cotton shirt and he helped her shrug out of it, his hands warm and sure. He was much more than a doctor, she guessed. He seemed to know a great deal about women's clothes fastenings.

At the moment, it was his experience as a doctor that she valued. His experience with women didn't matter a whit.

Chapter Four

Dr. James Callahan gallantly tipped his black felt top hat at the pretty young woman he met on the board sidewalk. "Mrs. Kirkland."

"Dr. Callahan! I was just thinking about stopping in to see you. It's about the baby."

A faraway look came into the elderly man's gray eyes. The first baby he had ever delivered scared the bejeesus out of him. Not because of the blood and the bruised and swollen flesh—he'd seen plenty of that in medical school—but because then, in his twenty-third year, he saw clearly what loving someone meant. A woman bravely—and sometimes not so bravely, he learned as he grew older—endured the agony of labor, risked her life to present her husband with a gift more costly, more treasured than anything on God's earth. His own sister, his niece Ellen's mother, had died bearing a child. James had never forgotten it.

"Nothing wrong with the baby, I hope?"

Mrs. Kirkland dimpled. "Far from it. Thad is thriving. Actually, it's my husband I am concerned about. He seems…different since the birth."

James understood instantly. A man hearing his wife's screams of agony for a day and half the night, a man who didn't stumble out to the barn and shoot himself, was changed forever by the experience. Sometimes James thought that's what had started his sister's husband with the drink. Ellen's father had let spirits destroy his life. It had almost destroyed her, as well.

"I wouldn't worry, Mrs. Kirkland. Husbands often feel pretty shaken by birth, just as much as the new mother. Maybe he's just realizing how precious you are to him."

Mrs. Kirkland seized his free hand. "Oh, thank you, Dr. Callahan. I think you are such a very wise man!" She squeezed his hand and pivoted away into Svensen's Mercantile.

Wise my ass. The love between a husband and wife had astounded him back then. He knew that no woman would ever feel that way about him. He'd always been painfully shy, and awkward around women. Different. Most men would rather play poker than spend their evenings reading Byron.

Twenty-five years ago he'd been a callow tenderfoot fresh out from the East, practicing his first year of medicine and dumb as an ox when it came to talking to a female without a stethoscope in his hand.

He had known this about himself for more than two decades. No sane woman would love him, would suffer and sacrifice for him the way he saw the wives of Willow Flat do for their men. All his life he'd been too awed by women to ever speak to one in anything other than a professional situation. Now he was forty-eight years old.

But Lord knew if a man never said good-morning to a lady, that man never got invited to afternoon tea. He got plenty of invites to down a slug or two of red-eye at the Wagon Wheel Saloon, but lately he felt a nagging hunger for something more. Something soft that smelled good. That smelled like lavender.

He'd waited all these years for Iona Everett, and time was growing short. If he didn't *do* something about it damn quick, he'd die a bachelor.

Near noon, Ellen heard Mr. Flint tramp up the stairs to her room, a tray with two plates of scrambled eggs and two mugs of coffee in his hands. The sun's rays beat at the bedroom window. Already the room was stifling; today would be a real scorcher.

She watched the man squeeze himself into her rocking chair and roll back and forth, nursing his coffee while she ate her breakfast. When she had eaten nearly all the eggs, she reached for her own mug on the bedside table and gulped down a large swallow.

Well! The man made excellent coffee, the best she'd ever tasted.

They sipped their coffee in silence until Mr. Flint set his mug on the plank floor, unfolded his long legs and ambled to the window. Without speaking, he drew the blue muslin curtains shut.

"What are you doing?" Her voice came out sharper than she intended.

"Hot in here. Be cooler if you block the sun."

"Oh." Of course. She was always up and out in the barn shortly after sunup, and she didn't come back upstairs until after dark. She couldn't remember when the last noontime had found her still in bed.

She turned her coffee mug around and around in her hands. "How long will I be laid up like this?"

His dark eyes met hers, an unnerving glint of amusement in their depths. "Long enough. Longer than you're going to like. Your bone has to knit before you put any weight on it."

Her fork clunked onto the plate. "How long?" she repeated.

He settled his rangy form back into the rocker, stretched out his legs and crossed his boots at the ankle. "I'd say you need a hired hand for the next few weeks."

Ellen choked on her coffee. "Weeks! I can't stay bedridden that long. My vegetables will shrivel up in this heat. The cow will go dry. The hens…" She had to keep the farm going, but he'd never understand her desperate need to do so.

He gave her a speculative look. "You want your leg to heal crooked? Have a limp the rest of your life?"

"Well, no." A sudden curiosity seized her. "Is that what happened to *your* leg?"

He said nothing.

"Mr. Flint? I asked you a question."

"I heard you. Could be I'm not going to answer it."

Irritation tightened her jaw. "And why is that?"

"Because it's none of your business," he said quietly.

Ellen bit her lip. "You're right, of course. I shouldn't have asked." But lordy-Lord, she couldn't lie here being an invalid, even for a few days. How would she water the vegetables and bake bread and churn butter and…all the other things that demanded her attention?

She set the mug aside and knotted her fingers together. "I can't pay you wages."

Mr. Flint's gaze met hers, his eyes hard as sapphires. "Didn't ask for any. I was thinking about meals and a place to sleep in your barn."

"Oh, no, I don't think—" The memory of the last wayfaring man she'd hired still made her stomach churn. But how would she manage without help?

"For how long?" She made her tone as crisp as she could.

The oddest look flitted across his face, instantly replaced by a carefully impassive expression. "Let's say for as long as it takes."

As long as it takes? Something about the way he said that made her uneasy. "I can ask the Gundersen boy to help out. He's chopped wood for me in the winter and last summer he helped bring in the hay."

"I'll be better than the Gundersen boy." Mr. Flint said it without apparent pride, just stated it as if he were saying, "Today is Tuesday."

"Besides," he added, "I want to stay."

Ellen opened her mouth without thinking. "Why?"

The rocking motion stopped abruptly. "You're one nosy woman, Miz O'Brian." He looked at her for a long minute, his eyes so stony she caught her breath.

"I know," she said with a sigh. "I guess it comes from being alone. I question everything. It is nosy, but

I need to be, well, careful. I don't much trust men, ever since Dan…"

"Yeah." He nodded once, downed the last of his coffee and set the mug on the floor beside him.

Ellen studied his face. He hid his feelings cleverly. Dollars to doughnuts there was something he wasn't telling her.

"Mr. Flint, you have not answered either of my questions."

"You're right." He rose, scooped his coffee mug off the floor, stacked her empty plate on his. "Maybe I'm tired of traveling. Maybe I want to stop somewhere and rest awhile."

He didn't look at her when he spoke.

Maybe. And maybe I'm the Queen of Sheba. Ellen smoothed out the sheet covering her lower torso.

"Anyway, Miz O'Brian, might be smart to say thanks, and wait till you're on your feet again. Right now you're in no position to run me off."

Ellen blinked. Was that a threat? She listened to the irregular rhythm of his footsteps going down the stairs. He was right about one thing: she did not want her leg to heal crooked.

It would make it even harder to hold on to the farm for when Dan returned. And if she had the child her heart yearned for, how would she tend it if she was crippled? It would be impossible to chase after a toddler if she couldn't walk right.

Ellen closed her eyes against the pain of her longing. It was foolish to hope for a child when her husband might be dead.

Downstairs, dishes clattered. The hand pump squeaked and water trickled into the sink. The back door opened, shut, then opened again. Later a rhythmic *thonk-thonk* carried on the still air, like an ax biting into a tree. She let the noises wash over her.

When she woke the sky was a milky lavender. Almost twilight. The curtains had been pushed back and the sash raised to catch the breeze. The soft squawks of her chickens drifted up from the yard. Bullfrogs croaked down by the creek, and the still, warm air smelled of dust.

She loved this place with its earthy smells, the warm, peaceful evenings and the mornings alive with inquisitive finches chattering in her apple trees. Her life moved forward in an ordered sequence of events, guided by the rising and setting of the sun. It was predictable. Safe.

It didn't matter that chores filled every hour between dawn and dark. The cow needed to be milked, the horse fed and the stall mucked out. The vegetables weeded, apples picked and cooked into applesauce… Oh, Lord, the drudgery never ended. Sometimes she felt as if she were suffocating.

But it would be worth it in the end. Dan would be so pleased when he returned, so proud of her. Something unforeseen must have happened to him that day he left for town. An accident, perhaps. Whatever it was, when he came home he'd find the farm prospering and his wife waiting with welcoming arms.

With a wrench she turned her mind away from Dan. She wouldn't allow herself to brood. She'd think about how peaceful it was just lying here in her bed, listening to the quiet noises she never had time to stop and enjoy—twittering finches in the pepper tree, Florence lowing across the meadow.

No sound came from downstairs. Maybe Mr. Flint had absconded with her horse and her cow, after all?

Don't be an idiot. If that rambling man had wanted either, he would have taken them this morning and not returned. True, he did take the horse, but he'd brought him back. Even so, it was hard to trust him. Even if he could set a broken leg.

By late afternoon Jess still tramped the perimeter of Ellen's farm. His shadow lengthened, but he had to learn the lay of the land. Stopping under the same spreading oak he'd climbed earlier, he knelt, unfolded a rumpled sheet of brown grocer's paper and wrestled a pencil stub out of his jeans pocket.

"Here, and here," he muttered. He marked the points with an X on the makeshift map, then sketched in the barn, the house, the creek and the pasture beyond it, the apple trees at the back of the property, even the tree under which he sat. Chewing the tip of the pencil, he studied the layout, then bent to draw a grid over the landmarks. Each square represented maybe five long strides. He'd start at the upper left boundary and me-thodically work his way across and then down. He'd cover every goddam inch of this ground before husband Dan came home.

By suppertime, Jess had milked Florence and locked the hens in their shelter. For the evening meal he boiled up an armload of sweet corn he'd picked, and heated a can of beans from her pantry. He dished up two plates, piling his own high with ears of corn, and clumped upstairs to Ellen's bedside.

He also carried with him the oak limb he'd cut and shaped this afternoon. By God, he was more nervous about what she'd think of that bit of wood than about his cooking.

Ellen heard him coming up the stairs, a clump and a pause, clump and pause. Balancing two steaming plates in his hands, he walked to the chiffonier and set them down next to the water basin.

"Got something for you," he said in a gravelly voice.

"Supper, so I see. That is good of you, Mr. Flint."

"Something besides supper." He unhooked an odd-shaped length of tree limb from his forearm and presented it for her inspection. "It's a crutch. I made it this afternoon."

Ellen stared at it. The wood had been cleverly shaped using the natural curve of the limb to fashion an underarm prop, padded with one of her clean dish towels. Her throat tightened.

She appreciated his gesture more than she could say.

She tried to smile, but her lips were trembly. "How very kind of you, Mr. Flint."

"It's a necessity, the way I see it. You need a way to get around, even if it's only as far as your wardrobe and the commode. Which, I assume, is under the bed?"

Her face flushed with heat. "It is." Surely they should not speak of such an intimate matter as her commode? It made her feel uneasy, as if he knew things about her she wished he didn't.

He laid the crutch at the foot of the bed and turned to the plates on the chiffonier. "You can try it out after supper."

He settled two pillows under her shoulders and laid another across her lap, pulled two forks out of his shirt pocket and handed her one. Her plate he settled on the lap pillow. Two ears of corn swam in a puddle of melted butter, and suddenly she was ravenous.

"I cannot imagine why I should be so hungry! All I've done is lie in bed all day." She lifted the corn and sank her teeth into the tender, sweet kernels, watching Mr. Flint settle into the rocker and begin to eat as well.

"Healing uses energy, just as much as baling hay. That's why you're hungry."

Ellen tipped her head to look at him. "You really are a doctor, aren't you?"

"Was one once, yes, as I told you. Sounds like you didn't believe me. I served four years, until—" He stopped abruptly.

"Until?"

"Until I stopped believing I could save anyone."

"Sometimes I don't know what I believe," Ellen heard herself say. She gnawed another two rows of kernels to hide her embarrassment. Butter dribbled down her chin but she didn't care. Corn on the cob had never tasted so good.

He sent her a penetrating look. "Why is that, Miz O'Brian?"

"It was clear once. Before Dan left. I believed in him. I believed in the farm, the land. In myself. I knew what my duty was as a wife."

She shouldn't be telling him this! But she'd kept the

fight between her duty and her feelings inside for so long she would burst if she didn't let out just a little bit of it. "Now, I…well, of course I still believe in the land."

Jess stopped rocking. "But not in yourself?"

She shook her head, then started on the second ear of corn on her plate. "Not so much anymore. Sometimes I have to ask myself…" She stopped, surprised at her need to talk about it. Surprised by the feelings she had kept locked up inside her.

He tipped the rocking chair forward. "You ever ask yourself what you will do if Dan doesn't come back? Why a woman like you is wasting her life waiting for a man who's been gone all these years?"

Her eyes widened. "Well, yes. I keep thinking one of these days he'll just walk in the gate, but it's been almost three years. I don't know how to *stop* waiting for him."

Jess nodded. "I wondered the same thing about my own life once. Nobody walked through *my* gate, so one day I got the bit in my teeth and walked through it myself. Left the army and came north."

With Callie. That's where everything started to go sour.

"I expect I am talking too much," Ellen said. Her cheeks grew pink as she forked up her beans. "I always talk to myself when I'm frightened or worried about something."

"Long conversations?" He didn't have the vaguest idea why he asked that, other than he was taken with the idea of her talking to herself. What did an almost-dried-up farm wife say to herself?

"Oh, not always. Sometimes I talk to Florence while I'm milking her. And the chickens, although they are terrible listeners."

Jess choked back a snort of laughter. Chickens. And Florence.

"Sometimes I even talk to my carrots and tomatoes. I tell them how proud I am that they grow so nicely."

Jess fastened his gaze on the plate of food in his lap. Her guileless confession was like a sharp stick poking at his heart.

"I'd say you're lonely, Miz O'Brian."

She said nothing for a long while. Finally she pushed her empty plate to one side of the lap pillow and laid her fork down alongside the two well-cleaned corncobs. "Mr. Flint, could I trouble you for a glass of water?"

Jess grinned. She sure could. He'd thought about his surprise most of the day. That is, when he wasn't busy mapping the property. Tipping the two corncobs from her plate onto his, he went downstairs, returning in a few moments with two glasses of cold liquid.

"Lemonade!" she exclaimed at the first taste. "Where did you—?"

"At the mercantile in town." The look of wonder and delight on her face pricked his chest in a way he hadn't expected.

She took two big swallows, sighed with pleasure and then skewered him with those eyes of hers. "You didn't steal the lemons, did you?"

"On the contrary. You paid for them." He waited for her to object, but she said not one word, just wrapped her hands around the cool glass and smiled.

"You don't know how long it's been since I've tasted lemonade."

He could guess. About as long as it had been since

she'd cranked up a batch of ice cream or had a new dress or danced at a social.

Or made love with a man.

Where had that come from? Ah, hell, it was obvious. She didn't have the look of a woman who ran loose; she tied up her hair at her neck and made do with chickens and a broken-down horse for company.

And then there was his own hunger, Jess admitted. The human male was simpleminded in some very basic ways. But he couldn't let that get in his way.

"You ready to try out the crutch?"

She drank the last of the lemonade and set the glass on the night table. "I guess I'm ready."

Jess studied her splinted right leg. "You'll have to sit up and swing your legs to the edge of the bed. Let your right one stick straight out, and don't try to bend it."

He settled his hands on her shoulders and pulled her up off the pile of pillows, then gently pivoted her body and eased her legs into position. He tried to shut out his awareness of her as a woman, how warm her skin felt, how good she smelled. Might be easier if she had more covering her than just her camisole and her drawers, especially with one leg split up to her thigh.

"Does it hurt?"

"Some. Not sharp and awful like it was before you set it. Just a steady ache."

"You cannot put any weight on that leg, Ellen. When you stand up, the crutch and your left leg will have to support you. You understand?"

She nodded. He positioned the crutch pad under her right armpit. Keeping his hands at her waist, he tugged her toward him until she stood upright. She swayed forward, but he tightened his grip to steady her.

"Take a step."

"I will if I can," she said. Her voice shook slightly, and he realized she was frightened. "Don't let go of me."

She plunked the crutch tip onto the floor and lurched toward him. Again he steadied her, but this time she was closer. So close he could smell her hair, a fragrance like roses and something spicy and clean. He loosened his grip at her waist, but kept his hands in place so she wouldn't fall.

She stumbled into him, then righted herself, breathing heavily. His own breathing was none too steady, he noted. The brief touch of her forehead against his chin, the smoky-sweet scent rising from her skin slammed into his gut like a 50-caliber bullet.

Instantly he lifted his hands from her body, but too late. He wanted to smell her, all of her. Taste her.

And more. His groin tightened.

Jess let out an uneven breath. What the hell was he thinking? There was something he had to do here, and the woman didn't matter. She damn well couldn't matter.

Chapter Five

It took Ellen a quarter of an hour to maneuver herself down the stairs using the crutch Mr. Flint had contrived for her. Settling one leg on the lower step and swinging the curved oak staff down to meet it, stair by stair, she managed a noisy descent, terrified that at any second she would land off balance and tumble to the bottom. But not even the ache in her injured leg dampened her determination. She had chickens to feed. She had herself to feed as well.

Moving around on only one good leg made her heart pound with exertion. By the time she reached the landing, her breath was heaving in and out in hoarse gasps. Now she knew why old Jeremiah Dowd, who had lost a leg during the War of the Rebellion, spent so many afternoons sitting under the leafy oak tree in the town square.

The first thing she saw when she stumped into the kitchen was her blue speckleware coffeepot on the still-warm stove. She lifted the lid and peeked in to find an almost full pot of rich-smelling brew. Four fresh eggs nestled in a china bowl, and the frying pan waited beside it. Thoughtful of the man. Either he was more civilized than she'd thought or he was after something.

But what? What would make a man like Mr. Flint take interest in the tiny farm she was working so hard to hold on to?

She broke the eggs into the bowl, whipped them into a froth with a fork and had just poured them into the butter-coated pan when she glanced out the window. Her hand froze on the spatula.

Mr. Flint stood in her yard, stirring something in her washtub, which sat over a fire pit he'd dug. With his shirt off he looked younger than she had supposed, his chest well developed, his back lean and tanned. She gazed at his smooth, bronzy skin and the V of fine dark hair that disappeared beneath his belt buckle until she felt her cheeks flush. With every movement of the peeled branch he used to stir the tub contents, sinewy muscles rippled in his shoulders.

Ellen slid the frying pan off the heat and clumped out onto the back porch. The hole in the screen door had been patched with a scrap of wire mesh. She didn't need reminding that there were zillions of such chores waiting to be addressed. Annoyed, she pushed the screen open with a slap. "What do you think you're doing?"

He poled the sudsy mass of pale-colored garments around the tub without looking up. "Washing clothes."

Steam rose into the hot morning air, making Ellen more acutely aware of the heat in the pit of her stomach. Heat she hadn't felt since Dan left.

"I usually do that in the shade. Yonder, by the pepper tree." She flinched at the accusatory tone in her voice. What was the matter with her? The man was doing her a favor, taking on work she couldn't manage at present.

He looked at her, shading his eyes with one hand. "Wasn't any sun when I started. Real pretty sunrise, though."

He'd started washing clothes at dawn? Ellen moved closer and peered down into the tub. She recognized the blue shirt he'd worn the day before, then the petticoat she'd muddied in the creek and the underdrawers he'd cut off her when he'd set her leg. Then another pair of what looked like men's drawers. No, two pairs.

His mouth quirked in a lazy, off-center smile. "Been awhile since my duds have seen hot water. I'm washing everything I own except the pants I'm wearing."

Heavens, did that mean under his tight-fitting jeans he wore no…no underwear? She stared at his crotch for an instant, then flicked her gaze to his mouth. Unlike his eyes, which revealed nothing, his mouth was extraordinarily expressive. She could practically read his mind from the position of his lips. At this moment, he was not thinking of his tub of washing; he was thinking of her!

Ellen swallowed hard. "Save the water. The creek's getting low, and my tomatoes are drying up."

"Got lye soap in it. You still want—"

"The tomatoes are over there, trained up on the chicken wire." Again, the words came out harsher than she intended.

"Yes, ma'am."

"The rinse water," she snapped. "Not the soapy. Pour

the soapy water on my honeysuckle vine next to the chicken house."

He studied her a moment longer than necessary, then shrugged his shoulders and resumed stirring the tub contents. The flush of heat in Ellen's face traveled down her neck and into her chest, as if a rush of hot, wet wind had curled about her.

She pivoted so fast the crutch under her armpit wobbled. "Excuse me, Mr. Flint. I have quite forgotten something."

Jess chuckled as she stumped away across the yard. "Call me Jess, why don't you?" he said to her back.

She kept moving. "Why should I?"

"Because it looks like I'll be here for a while." He chuckled again as the screen door snapped shut. He could tell she didn't like the idea much.

That was fine with him. In a funny way he didn't much like the idea, either, even though it was what he'd planned. It wasn't that he didn't enjoy her company, because he did. She had a crispness about her, a strength he found intriguing. She worked hard. The vegetable garden flourished, the cow was healthy, the horse well cared for. She even had a well-scrubbed kitchen floor. It could not have been easy for her alone all this time, but it sure was plain she wasn't a quitter. She had courage and she had grit. He wondered if husband Dan knew what he'd thrown away when he rode off.

Ellen O'Brian had two other things Jess would give his right arm for—the respect of the townspeople and the ability to laugh at herself. Rare qualities for a woman in these circumstances. Downright admirable. He wished he didn't have to hurt her to get what he wanted.

For a moment he considered stripping and tossing his jeans into the tub, then discarded the idea. It might spook her so bad she'd run him off, and no matter how dirt-encrusted or sweat-sticky his trousers, he couldn't take the risk.

He watched the soapy water bubble around his underdrawers and her petticoat. Entwined together in a sudsy knot, the garments writhed in a sinuously suggestive dance, and suddenly he remembered the satiny skin of her thigh when he'd cut her lace-trimmed drawers away. His fingers tightened on the stirring pole. Better keep his mind on her tomatoes.

And on his most important task of the day—searching another small area of O'Brian land.

When the clothes looked reasonably clean, he dragged the tub of water off the fire and over to the chicken house, tipping it out where the honeysuckle vine wound up the wall and spilled over the roof. A honeysuckle vine on a chicken house, of all things. On the privy, too, he noted. He'd save a gallon or so of water for that one as well.

Rinsing was easier. And cooler. He pumped fresh water into the tub, and after he'd kicked dirt over his coals and wrung out all the rinsed garments, he scouted for a clothesline hook. On his circuit around the yard he glimpsed a blur of blue through the kitchen window.

She wore another one of her husband's shirts, a plain blue chambray. Most women would look dowdy in such a getup, but even though the shoulder seams drooped off her slim form and she'd rolled the sleeves up to her elbows, the oversize garment made her look female as hell. He'd bet she didn't know that. Or maybe she didn't care what she looked like.

Jess halted. He'd never met a woman who didn't care about her appearance. Was saving this farm for her scoundrel of a husband more important to her than how she felt as a woman?

The thought nagged at the back of his brain until he found the clothesline loop at the side of the house and ran a rope to the pepper tree some yards away. He lugged over the tub of clean, wet clothes and began to drape the garments over the line.

First her lace-trimmed underdrawers. Carefully he shook the wrinkles from the garment and then, unable to suppress the urge, he stood looking at it. The warm breeze caught the underside and belled the drawers out. The leg he'd had to slit flapped in the current of air; maybe she could mend it on the treadle sewing machine he'd seen in her parlor.

He ran one finger down the seam. It was all that lacy edging that fascinated him. She sure as hell cared what she wore *underneath* her sturdy work skirt and Dan's old shirt. On impulse, he brought the soft white fabric to his nose and inhaled. Beneath the clean smell of laundry soap floated a faint flowery scent. He breathed in again, deeper, and almost choked at the sound of her voice.

"Clothespins," she said. She thrust a striped denim drawstring sack at him and shook it once so it rattled. The sound reminded him of the collection of chicken wishbones he'd treasured as a boy. Funny thing to treasure, maybe, but knowing he had a chance for even one of his wishes to come true had kept him going. Jess wished he had one of those wishbones now, just for luck.

With an effort he jerked his thoughts back to the laundry. "Thanks."

She stood looking at him, dropped her gaze to the underdrawers in his hand and then perused the line he'd rigged.

"I should be thanking you, Mr. Flint. I don't believe I could manage hanging out clothes balancing on my crutch."

"Don't even try," he ordered. "If you fall, I'll have another load of washing to do."

A glimmer of a smile touched her mouth. "I try never to take on more than I can manage."

"Seems to me running this farm might be more than you can manage. And don't 'Mr. Flint' me. Name's Jess. Short for Jason."

Her eyes widened and he could have bit his tongue off. Hell, she must have heard of Jason Flint. Half the sheriffs west of the Mississippi had his picture plastered all over their walls.

"Very well, then. Jess." She looked at him curiously and Jess's gut tightened. If she did recognize him, she could go for the sheriff.

But she couldn't ride. She couldn't even walk very far. Besides, maybe she hadn't flinched because of his name; might be something else that made those unnerving, clear blue eyes look so big. Maybe his photograph wasn't on the sheriff's wall in Willow Flat.

"You going to wave my smalls around until they're dry?" she inquired, a bite in her tone.

"Uh…guess not, ma'am."

"Then stop staring at them and hang 'em up. There are other chores to do."

Jess obeyed, pinning the lace-edged garment to the line, then shaking out her wet petticoat.

"Hang that upside down," she instructed. "Stretch the hem out so it'll dry faster."

Without a word, he did as she asked. While he secured seven clothespins along the bottom of edge of her petticoat, she leaned on her crutch and fidgeted. When he turned back to the tub of wet clothes, he caught her looking at him. Goddam if her eyes seemed to get more penetrating every time they met his.

Jess swallowed. "What other work do you need done today?"

"Tiny needs fresh hay in his stall, and that means shoveling out the manure."

"Easy enough. Then what?"

"You won't like it." She said it with a half smile on her lips.

"Okay, I won't like it." He watched her eyes turn sparkly as she studied him.

"You hired me, Miz O'Brian. I do what you say, even if I don't like it." When she opened her mouth, he braced himself.

"There's a town social on Sunday. I want you to help me bake a cake."

He'd forgotten he'd promised Svensen he'd remind her of the social. Ah, hell, what difference did it make if it had slipped his mind? It hadn't slipped *hers*.

"A cake," he said, his voice flat.

"A spice cake, flavored with anise. I've made it for the social every year since I was tall enough to reach the oven door." Every year since Mama had died.

"What's so difficult about it that you need help?"

She sent him such a withering look he felt his throat go dry. "I can't beat cake batter five hundred strokes and hold on to this crutch at the same time."

She inspected the last garment remaining in the washtub—his blue shirt—and raised her eyes as far as the clothesline. "Let's muck out the barn first while your shirt dries. I am not sure I want a half-naked man in my kitchen."

Her cheeks, he noted, were tinged a soft rosy pink. "Who's going to know?" he retorted. "Seems to me what you do in the privacy of your own house is…private."

Ellen pursed her lips and tipped her head to one side. "*I* will know."

Jess grinned. "Some folks are proper only when other folks are looking. Then there are some, maybe like you, with a moral code they carry on the inside."

"I should hope so, Mr. Flint. Otherwise people can get confused sorting out what is right from what is wrong. Don't you agree?"

Her words sounded mighty sensible. In a way he envied her clarity. He'd never found it that easy. Even now he was deliberating on how far he would go before his conscience stopped him.

"Mr. Flint?" She gestured with her head. "The barn?"

He didn't expect her to plod laboriously after him all the way to Tiny's stall, but she did. The blast of heavy heat inside the barn made him feel as if he were walking into an oven. Jess left the door propped open for fresh air, then grabbed a pitchfork and started in.

While he worked, Ellen unlatched the gate and walked the big plow horse out of his stall. Between scrapes of the shovel and the sound of manure thunking into the wheelbarrow, Jess could hear her talking to the animal.

"Come on, you sweet old thing." Out of the corner of his eye he watched her teeter on the crutch as she stroked the animal's nose. "It's only for a little while, and then you'll have nice, clean straw to roll in."

"Roll in!" Jess bit off a snort of disbelief. "Stall's not big enough for him to turn around in, let alone roll."

"But he doesn't know that," Ellen cooed at the animal. "He has no idea what I'm saying, he just likes the sound of my voice." She leaned her cheek against the horse's huge shoulder. "Some things don't need any words, do they, Tiny?"

"Some animals are smarter than others, all right," Jess stated.

Ellen smiled up at the animal. "Tiny's not smart. He just knows I love him."

Jess leaned on his shovel and watched her make eyes at the plow horse. He liked hearing the soft murmur of her voice as she talked to the animal. Kinda touching, in a way. She talked to her chickens, too. Even her tomato plants. She must get damn lonely out here all by herself.

He resumed shoveling up the dirty straw until an unbidden thought drilled him between the eyes. *You can't afford to feel sympathy for her.* That would be just plain stupid. He couldn't afford to feel *anything* for her.

He straightened abruptly and looked the plow horse

in the eye. *She's got you eating out of her hand, hasn't she, old fella?*

Immediately the animal's ears flattened. *No need to be jealous, now. Only one male on this spread is going to let that happen, and it's not me.*

Ellen rested on the bale of clean hay until Mr. Flint motioned that he was ready to cut the baling wire and fork the straw into Tiny's stall. With an awkward lurch she stood up and managed to hobble to the barn door. She felt light-headed and out of breath in the heat. She prayed she would make it back to the kitchen before she collapsed.

The clank of metal told her Mr. Flint had finished and was returning the shovel and the pitchfork to the rack against the wall. She started across the yard, heard him shut the barn door and tramp after her.

"Tired?" His voice jarred her concentration.

"Yes. More than I thought I'd be."

He caught up to her and slowed his steps to stay by her side. "It's hard work, learning a new way to walk."

Ellen shot him a glance. "Is that what you had to do?"

"Up to a point. My leg didn't heal right." A tightening of his lips alerted her to an unease he kept well hidden.

"Where were you when you hurt your leg?"

"In a Confederate prison. Richmond. I escaped, but I had to rip the plaster off my leg to do it."

"Was it worth it? Your freedom in exchange for a crippled leg?"

His face changed. "Wasn't a choice, really. Grew me up damn fast."

"It must have been painful."

"Yeah. But if I'd stayed, they'd have broken the other one, too."

Ellen's insides recoiled, but she said nothing. Instead she focused on keeping her balance as she lurched toward the back porch. Mr. Flint stayed at her elbow, but he let her negotiate the steps on her own. By the time they reached the kitchen, she was out of breath again.

She sank onto a ladder-back chair, closed her eyes and fanned herself with her apron. Mr. Flint leaned over her.

"You all right?"

"Oh, right enough. Just winded." When she opened her eyelids a glass of water sat on the table before her, and he had settled his long frame onto the chair across from her.

At first she tried very hard not to look at his bare chest. After an awkward silence, she gave up. She liked looking at his tanned, well-muscled torso, even slicked with perspiration and smudged with dirt. It would be an experience to bake her cake with a half-dressed helper.

"I'll go wash up and get my shirt off the clothesline. Should be dry by now."

"I would offer to iron it for you, but…"

"Doesn't need ironing, Ellen. Don't need to get fancied up to make a cake."

A flicker of regret teased at her.

At the back door, he turned and held her gaze with an expression she couldn't read. Not concern, exactly. Just a kind of awareness. Recognition.

Ellen swallowed over a lump the size of an egg and stood to fetch her blue mixing bowl.

Chapter Six

Inside the consulting room in his office, Dr. James Callahan set his hat on the shelf, shed his summer linen jacket and loosened his tie. Part of him hated getting gussied up just to walk past the boardinghouse each morning. But another part of him, the part that had tumbled head-over-coattails in love twenty-five years ago, wanted to see her again.

He had watched Iona Everett since the year she had turned seventeen, the year he had come out to Willow Flat at his sister's request. Iona had grown from a shy, soft-spoken girl into a lushly beautiful young woman who played the piano and taught Sunday school. Then, at twenty-two, she had married town banker Thaddeus Everett, and Doc Callahan's heart had slowly turned to stone. Not even doting on his sister's surviving child, Ellen, over the years had assuaged the hurt.

Twelve years later, Iona had been widowed, and Doc resumed his morning walks past the tree-shaded, three-story home she'd turned into a boardinghouse. Today she had been sitting in a white wicker chair on the wide front veranda, a vision in lavender dimity. She must be in her early forties now, Doc thought. She looked no more than thirty, her skin still satin-smooth, her amber-colored hair kissed with silver.

He'd tipped his black top hat, and when she slowly inclined her head in response, as she always did, he had hurried on by, his tongue too tangled to speak.

Now he hung his jacket on the hook behind the consulting room door and closed his eyes in disgust. *What ails you, man? You'd think you'd never seen a pretty woman before!*

Oh, that he had, many times. Always the same pretty woman. Iona. Even her name was beautiful.

With a sigh Doc straightened the stack of medical journals on his crammed desk and readied his office for the first patient of the day. *Physician, heal thyself!*

All afternoon he would rehearse what he would say to her, and tomorrow morning, he resolved, instead of just tipping his hat and striding on down the street, he would muster up his courage and speak to her.

Jess dangled the ruffly white apron from one thumb and faced Ellen. "Last time I wore an apron, it was waterproof linen and I was taking off a man's leg. I feel ridiculous in this frilly little bit of—"

"Put it on," she ordered. "Unless you like getting flour dusted all over your front." Against her will, her gaze flicked to his well-worn jeans. The thought of his lean, hard body encased in her soft feminine garment made her grin. "'Course, you don't *have* to." She tried hard not to laugh.

"What's so funny?" he demanded.

She raised her eyes, worked to keep them riveted on the second button of his shirt. She couldn't tell him. Putting her apron on a man like him was like spreading frosting on a tree stump. "Your shirt is still damp," she improvised.

"Bet it's cooler than yours. It's hot in here, and it'll be worse when we stoke up the fire in the stove."

He slipped the neck band over his head and tied the apron strings behind him. "Look at me." He shook his head in disbelief at what he was doing. As a final gesture he fluffed out the ruffled hem.

Ellen laughed out loud. "You look quite fetching."

"Feel damn silly if you want the truth."

"Who's going to know, Mr. Flint? We're private. You said so yourself not ten minutes ago."

He shot her a withering look. Ellen's heart doubled its beat until she saw the corners of his lips twitch. When the telltale twitch blossomed into a real smile, her heart skittered again. His sharp, hawklike face relaxed when he smiled. And those wary, dark blue eyes lost the hungry look that made her so curious about him. When his eyes softened, something different shone in their depths. Something arresting. She liked his face when he smiled.

She grabbed her red painted receipt box and thumbed through the slips of paper. "You will find butter in the cooler. Sugar's in the small barrel, flour in the big one."

With a sideways look he eyed the swinging door she indicated, then returned his gaze to her. "How much of each?"

She pretended to read the recipe, though she knew the ingredients and the measurements by heart. For some reason she needed to be doing something with her hands. A smiling Jason Flint made her even more uneasy.

"One teacup-size lump of butter, two of brown sugar, three of flour. Take two bowls. Put the butter and the sugar in together."

He gathered up two china mixing bowls from the shelf next to the stove and disappeared into the pantry. She heard him open the sugar barrel, then the flour barrel, which had a cover so tight-fitting it squeaked. He emerged with a bowl in each hand; in one, a glob of butter the size of his fist rode on a mound of brown sugar.

"What next?" he said as he plunked the bowls on the table.

"Cream the butter and the sugar."

He cocked his head at her and frowned. "Cream? You didn't tell me to get cream."

Ellen laughed out loud. "You don't need cream. That just means to mix the butter and the sugar together. Here, use a fork."

He took the utensil offered and began to squash the ball of butter into the sugar. Something about the way he used the fork, slowly pressing it down through the soft butter, then lifting the sugar up from the bottom of the bowl, sent an odd thrill into her belly. His hands—that was it. His fingers moved with deliberation at the task, his motions unhurried and thorough.

He walked the same way, Ellen thought. Loose-limbed and sure of himself, as if he were stalking something. She wrenched her gaze away and began cracking eggs into a soup bowl.

"Three eggs," she said, just to make a noise in the suddenly quiet room. "When the butter and sugar are mixed, dump in the eggs. Then I'll beat it while you sift the flour."

He nodded, still frowning, and pushed the bowl of butter and sugar within her reach. She stirred the contents smooth, then started on the first hundred strokes with the wooden spoon. It was hard to do while seated; after fifty strokes, her arm ached and she gave it up.

"Baking soda," she announced when he looked at her for instruction. "Then add some spices to the flour. Cinnamon and nutmeg and crushed anise seeds." She pointed to the small savories cabinet hanging on the wall next to the sink. "A teaspoonful of each."

His care in measuring out the spices struck her as unusual. Few men would proceed with such delicacy, spilling nothing, gently grinding the anise with her mortar and pestle. The rich scent of licorice filled the warm kitchen. Anise always sent her imagination flying away to far-off places that smelled of exotic spices— ginger and cardamom—instead of farm dust. She closed her eyes and breathed deeply.

"Tired?"

"Certainly not. I have four hundred more strokes to do after you mix in the flour and a little buttermilk and some vanilla extract. *Then* I will be tired."

"How much is 'a little buttermilk'?" His look of genuine puzzlement touched her. A man like him was a fish out of water in a kitchen. But he was trying, she'd give him that.

"Just enough so it looks right," she said gently. "The amount's different every time. Cooking is an inexact art, Mr. Flint."

"Yes, ma'am." He squinted over the measuring, working his lower lip between his teeth as he dipped the spoon and leveled the spices off with his forefinger. Completely absorbed in the task, he seemed unaware of Ellen's sharp perusal of his face until he glanced up suddenly and his eyes met hers.

An unspoken question appeared in his gaze, but he said nothing. Instead, he raised one dark eyebrow in a rakish challenge of some sort.

A wave of dizziness swept over her. The heat. The spice-scented air in the kitchen. The smell of the man's body as he bent near and set the mixing bowl before her. Soap and sweat and something else. She flushed crimson, from the V below her neck where she'd left Dan's shirt unbuttoned, all the way up to her hairline.

She kept her eyes on the bowl of cake batter and counted her strokes. At three hundred fifty-seven, her arm gave out.

"Finished?" he asked.

"Close enough. Butter those two round tins and see if the oven's ready."

"How do I tell when it's—"

"Stick your hand in for a count of four. If you can't make it to four, it's hot enough."

"An inexact art," he muttered. "Like you said."

"I find that very little in life is clear-cut," Ellen responded. "The Lord does not seem to understand 'exact.'"

Jess caught a flicker of some emotion that crossed her face and just as quickly disappeared. Regret. And a generous dose of bitterness. She'd been through a lot, managing without Dan. Even a strong woman would break eventually. He wondered how long she would last.

At her direction, he poured the batter into the tin cake pans, dropped them sharply on the surface of the stove "to break up air bubbles," and slid them onto the oven rack. When he straightened, he noticed Ellen was nodding sleepily over the mixing bowl where she'd been swiping her finger for a taste.

"Go out onto the front porch," he ordered. "Get some air."

She struggled to her feet, grasped the crutch and clumped into the parlor. "I'll do the washing up later," she called as she opened the front door.

He heard the screen door swish shut, then the rhythmic creak of the willow rocker. Jess sat down in the chair she had vacated. His eyes glued to the oven door, he began to count the minutes before his cake would be done.

Ellen awoke when a laden dinner plate settled into her lap and a low, raspy voice said, "Thought you might be hungry."

Jess leaned over her, one hand on the back of the willow rocker, the other steadying the plate on her thighs. The musky male scent of his body jerked her heart into an uneven rhythm.

"That was thoughtful of you, bringing my lunch out here."

"More like supper. Look." He tipped his head toward the flaming sky in the west.

Ellen stared past his shoulder at the peach-and-purple clouds on the horizon. "My chickens," she murmured. "The cow…my cake! Oh for Lord's sake, I forgot all about it. It'll be burned to cinders by now." She started to rise, then remembered the plate on her lap.

"I milked," Jess said quickly. He caught the plate as it slid toward her knees. "Fed the chickens. Took in the washing."

He didn't tell her what else he'd done while she slept. Didn't tell her he'd combed a five-square-foot piece of her farmland until his knees ached and the back of his neck got sunburned.

"What about the cake? I can't attend the social without my cake!"

Jess shook his head. Women took the smallest things so seriously. "The cake," he began. He almost said "my" cake, but caught himself in time. A woman might take usurpation of a cake extra seriously.

"The cake is cooling in the kitchen. Looks pretty near perfect if I do say so myself."

"It ought to be," Ellen said. "I've been winning prizes for thirteen years. Fourteen counting this year."

He gave her a quick, interested look. "You live here all your life?"

"In town, yes. We bought the farm after my father died, four years ago."

"I take it winning is important to you?"

She thought about that for a full minute. "It didn't used to be. It didn't much matter until I got old enough to understand why the town folks shunned me. After that I couldn't stand not winning."

"Why—?"

"Because of my father," she said quickly. "He wasn't much liked when he was alive. He…drank."

"What about Dan, your husband? Did the town folks—"

"Dan has nothing to do with it." But the tightness in her voice told Jess something else. Her standing in the Willow Flat community had been based on her actions, not Dan's. For that, Jess was glad. She'd built a life here. He wanted to leave her that.

Ellen studied the plate of food on her lap. Two hard-cooked eggs, cut into quarters. Slices of red, juicy tomatoes, a wedge of cheese and two pieces of her day-old brown bread, thickly buttered.

"Too hot in the kitchen to cook," Jess muttered.

"I see you found my tomato vines." In a soft voice she added, "I am proud of my tomatoes."

"Irrigated with wash water, like you said. At least that's what I think I used."

Ellen laughed. "They'll probably taste like soap."

"They'll taste like tomatoes."

Her smile faded. "I try not to think about the way of nature. The Lord giveth and the Lord taketh away. Mostly he taketh away. He must have missed my tomatoes." She popped a section of boiled egg into her mouth.

"You sound like you've picked a good quarrel with the Lord."

"I am plenty mad at him at present. I will still be mad at him when they lay me in my grave."

Jess knew better than to pursue the matter further; he'd get her riled up and she'd be hard to handle, riled up. He studied the dark shadows beneath her eyes, her work-worn hands, the pulse throbbing at the curve of her throat. Ellen O'Brian was a fighter. He had to admire that.

But she wasn't going to win. A sour taste rose in his mouth and he swallowed hard. "About this social tomorrow…"

"What about it?" she asked over a mouthful of tomatoes. "It's the Fourth of July, always a big town wingding. I never miss it."

"Think you could sit a horse?"

Her face changed. "Guess I'll have to if I want to go."

"There's a doctor in town, right?"

"Yes, my uncle, Dr. James Callahan. Why? Are you ailing?"

"Thought he might put a plaster on your broken leg. A plaster cast is easier to walk around on than a splinted limb."

Her face lit up as if somebody had turned up a lamp flame inside her. "Then maybe I could even join in the dancing. That's the best part of the social."

"Maybe. First have to figure out how to get you there." He'd think it over later, after she went to bed. "You got something else needs doing tonight?"

"Boiling up my cake frosting. Just butter and sugar and some cold coffee. They call it Araby icing. Takes exactly seven minutes from start to finish, but you have to keep stirring it. Do you think you could…?"

"Thought you'd never ask," Jess said dryly.

"Thought I'd let you wear my apron again, too," she said with a laugh.

"Thanks."

"Mr. Flint?"

"Yes, Mrs. O'Brian?"

"Think you could also manage to iron my clean petticoat? The one you washed this morning?"

"I guess if you can ride a horse with your leg splinted, I can figure out how to iron your petticoat."

"Mr. Flint?" she said again. This time her blue eyes pinned him where he stood.

"Yes, Mrs. O'Brian?"

"There's some reason why you're here. I want to know what it is."

Jess looked away toward the purpling sky. "First off, it's plain you need help. You can't keep up the chores with a broken leg."

She nodded, but when he turned his head toward her she sought his gaze again. "And second?"

"Second…" He drew in a full breath and exhaled. "Maybe I'm…looking for something."

The instant the words were out he knew he'd said too much. The trick to lying was to stick close to the truth, up to a point. But she was the kind of woman who looked beneath the surface of things. Sooner or later, she'd smell him out.

"Looking for what?"

"Looking for…maybe some place to catch my breath for a while. Maybe a place that needs me." Both statements were true; he just wasn't telling her all of it.

And Lord, deep down he hoped she never found out the rest.

Chapter Seven

Exhausted from climbing the stairs step by agonizingly slow step, Ellen tottered into her blue-wallpapered bedroom, plopped down on the bed and began unbuttoning her shirt. Her broken leg ached. Her hands shook with fatigue. In the summer heat, just moving from the stove to the kitchen table made her pant with effort.

An hour ago she'd given up and instructed Mr. Flint in making her Araby frosting. Unless she was mistaken, he had actually enjoyed it, especially licking the spoon.

Raising her arms and twisting awkwardly, she managed to remove her skirt, then her petticoat and camisole. Thank goodness she hadn't worn her corset. But if she attended the social, she'd have to wear it. Respectable women just didn't dispense with proper undergarments.

She groaned aloud. Another reason not to attend.

She moved laboriously to the window, opened it as wide as it would go and drank in the warm night air. It was still light out, yet it must be near nine; she could hear the raggedy old rooster herding his harem of squawking hens onto their roosts for the night. The clucking noises finally subsided, and then she heard a voice floating up in the quiet air.

She couldn't make out the words, but the timbre of his voice and the slow, meandering tune stirred something inside her. Loneliness. And an odd yearning. She preferred lively music, fiddle music played fast. Otherwise, she sank into sadness and it took a day or two to work herself out of it.

She wouldn't listen, she decided. Flopping down on top of the sheet, she closed her eyes and tried to blot out his voice.

"'Been runnin' all my life, That's why I have no wife. Been near enough to hell to smell the smoke....'"

The song made her hurt inside. Made her think about the path she'd set out for herself and the long uphill pull it was turning out to be. Dan *would* be proud of her, provided she lived long enough to see him again. Each day that passed, she grew more respectable, and more weary, and his memory grew more faded. Sometimes she couldn't recall his features clearly, as if he were dead and buried. Still, was he not her husband? Had she not vowed to cleave to him until death?

He used to be the most important person in her life, but lately large chunks of time passed when she didn't think of him at all. Instead, she focused on milking Florence and setting broody hens, plowing the cornfield, planting alfalfa, wrestling shocks of hay into the barn. So many, many things that had less and less to do with Dan as time dragged by.

"'Been ridin' through this land, for another cowboy's brand, and now I'm just an old man goin' broke....'"

"I wish to God he'd stop singing!" she breathed.

Then the image of Mr. Flint swathed in her ruffled white apron popped into her mind. She saw him bent over the double boiler, stirring lazy figure eights in the bubbling sugar mixture with a wooden spoon, swirling his forefinger in the frosting bowl, grinning like a mischievous boy. Now she pictured him on her front porch, sprawled in the rocker, singing to the fat, gold summer moon.

The man was dangerous. She sensed it as clearly as if he'd said so outright. He wanted something. Needed something from her.

Ellen let a soft groan escape. She didn't want to admit she was both wary and intrigued by him. And right now, *she* needed something from *him*—his legs, and the strong arms of a hired hand.

She had no choice right now but to play the game, use the man for her purposes and hope her leg healed before he got around to *his* purpose.

She rested one hand on her midriff, felt her indrawn breath lift her flesh, then settle it, like the rising and falling of the sea tide. It wouldn't be too difficult to have him around for a short while. Despite the hard edge she sensed about the man, she rather liked him.

When Ellen stepped out the back door on Sunday morning, Jess blinked and took a second look, and then a third. She looked like a slice of summer sunshine in a flowered yellow dress made of some soft-looking fabric that hugged her bosom, nipped in at her waist and flared over her hips with just the right amount of fullness. His mouth went dry. The wide-brimmed straw hat, trimmed with yellow ribbon, hid her face.

She limped toward him using the crutch he'd made, keeping her eyes on the ground. Her cheeks reddened with the effort of moving.

"Good morning," he called over a catch in his throat. "Wait there." He led the big plow horse closer to her.

"Good morning." Her smile told him everything. She'd slept well, eaten the breakfast he'd left for her, and was itching to get the cake to her July social. *His* cake. If it won a prize, he wanted some of the glory.

"Pretty dress," he said. He gave her a slow once-over, from the toes of her black leather lace-ups to the top of her head, where she'd pinned the straw hat at a rakish angle. "Makes you look real…" he searched for a word that wouldn't put her in a huff "…womanly."

She flashed him her no-nonsense look. "Since I am female, that is not surprising." Her voice sounded frosty as a December night.

Jess swallowed a chuckle. She was female and then some. That too-big man's shirt she favored sure hid her assets under a proverbial bushel. Maybe that's why she wore it. Ellen O'Brian seemed unaware of how strikingly handsome she was. Not delicate. Not just pretty, with puffed out skirts and ruffles on her petticoat, but downright beautiful.

As a matter of fact, everything about this woman was surprising. *Danny boy, what a goddam fool you are.*

She stood near the horse's head, breathing hard from her exertion. "How am I going to mount?"

"I'll lift you up. You can carry the cake tin on your lap."

She nodded once and faced him. Carefully he closed his hands around her waist and instantly felt the rigid corset stays under her dress. How the devil had she managed to lace it up by herself? Or maybe it opened in the front? The picture that rose in his mind made him swallow and look away.

Ellen caught her bottom lip between her teeth as her body was lifted off the ground and settled sideways on Tiny's broad back. Her bottom was cushioned by folded blankets, but her splinted leg stuck straight out.

"Hold on, now." Jess handed her the covered cake tin, then mounted behind her and slung her crutch alongside, like a rifle scabbard. He lifted the reins. "Gee-yap."

Tiny took a step forward, and Ellen's stiffly upright body swayed toward him. He knew she wouldn't fall off; he had one arm across her middle, the other, holding the reins, almost touching her rigid back. He concentrated on loosening his hold, and clicked his tongue at the horse.

The animal's lumbering, uneven gait unbalanced her again. Her shoulder pushed against his chest. Instantly she straightened, but Tiny's next step rocked her against Jess once more.

This time he brought his palm to her shoulder and held her immobile. He kept his hand in place long enough to get his idea across, and after a moment she stopped trying to sit up straight and let herself lean sideways against him.

"Good girl," he murmured. "Safer this way." He bent his head, avoiding her hat brim, and inhaled deeply. The scent of her hair reminded him of flowers. Sweet ones.

"I should think it would be *less* safe," she said in a crisp voice.

Jess chuckled. "I was thinking of stability. Staying seated on the horse. You…" he paused to glance down at her chin, just visible under the straw bonnet "…were thinking of something else?"

She made no answer, and when she tried to lean away from him he touched her shoulder once more. "Relax, Mrs. O'Brian. You're a married woman."

"Exactly," she snapped. "Keep that in mind."

"Oh, I keep it in mind, all right. Fact is, it's occupying more of my attention than I'd bargained for."

"Just how do you mean that?"

Now he detected an icy edge to her tone. She sure didn't mince words. Nor did she shy away from asking direct questions, especially ones he wasn't prepared to answer.

"I mean I am aware of your marital status." He did not add that he tried hard not to think about it.

She said nothing for at least a mile, and when she did speak, the words punched into his gut like a barbwire belt.

"You have a sly, silky-tongued way about you, Mr. Flint. I wonder that you are not in some way on the shady side of the law."

There was a long silence while another mile slipped past.

"If you must know," Jess said at last, "I cheat at cards. You found me out without playing a single hand."

Another stretch of quiet ensued.

"That," she finally said in a schoolteachery voice, "is because I cheat at cards myself."

"You're lying," Jess said softly.

She tipped her head and sent him a penetrating look. "So are you."

Her statement shoved him into the barbwire again. Before he could regroup, they rounded a bend and the town came into view. Just one main street, with false-fronted wooden buildings painted a uniform blinding white; a grassy, tree-covered square across from the redbrick courthouse; side streets with pretty gardens fronting clapboard houses. Jess tightened his lips. It was the kind of place he no longer belonged in.

Within minutes a gaggle of chattering children in pinafores and overalls surrounded the big plow horse.

"Miss Ellen!"

"Tiny!"

The tribe of youngsters escorted them like royalty into Willow Flat, population 1,734.

"Looks like we'll have to continue this conversation later," he murmured.

She lifted her head and sent a bolt of blue-eyed lightning straight into his eyes. "We most certainly will."

Doc Callahan wrapped the wet plaster and gauze cast around his niece's broken leg, patted her shoulder when it was over and offered her a peppermint stick. "Should be walkin' on it in about three weeks, Ellen. You just relax and enjoy the time off."

"Three weeks!"

The gray-bearded physician inclined his head. "Yup. Could be worse. The splint helped, and that crutch, too. That hired man of yours has a mighty good doctoring instinct. You be sure to tell him that."

She would tell him no such thing. Jess Flint was puffed up enough as it was over "his" cake and "his" Araby frosting. She sniffed. The man hadn't even known how to grease a cake pan when he started. Men could be so...so territorial at times.

At other times, the human male was a complete mystery. Dan, for instance. Even Uncle James. She knew he was lonely. And she knew he had loved Iona Everett since the first day he came to town. Now that she'd been widowed, why hadn't he spoken for her?

Jess Flint was a mystery as well. Something about him drew her, stirred her nerves into spaghetti, and at the same time warned her to keep her distance.

Despite the awkwardness of the new plaster cast, she made her way out of her uncle's office and down the board sidewalk with considerably more ease than before. She still needed the crutch for balance while she hobbled along, but her whole body felt lighter.

Maybe it was wearing a dress again. She didn't do it very often. She wondered suddenly why she didn't; it surely did lift her spirits.

When she reached the grassy picnic area, Jess announced that he had taken "his" cake over to the dessert table; all she had to do was relax and enjoy herself, like Doc said.

Ellen bit back a laugh. "In that case, I'll have a great big plate of potato salad and a cool glass of lemonade with the church ladies, over there under the shady oak tree." Lord, it would be heavenly to eat something she herself hadn't grown, or cooked, or both.

She liked potato salad so much she wouldn't mind

listening to the gossipy Presbyterian women. As usual, they would talk-talk-talk, and she would eat.

"…And," Caroline Svensen added in an undertone, "I heard later that she was…"

Six bonneted heads bent forward as the mercantile owner's wife lowered her voice. Ellen, now the seventh lady in the circle of discreetly covered petticoats and dress-up shoes, sat unmoving on the warm grass, her gaze on Caroline but her fork making its way back and forth from her plate to her mouth. She didn't care who had promised or betrayed or compromised whom; she wanted to enjoy the heaping plate Emma Knowles had brought her.

"You'll pop your buttons," the sprightly older woman had announced. "Don't see how a body can eat like that and stay so skinny."

It was easy, Ellen thought. She feasted only twice a year, at Easter and the Fourth of July. The rest of the time her suppers were meatless and meager. Once in a while Cy Gundersen from the neighboring farm sent over a ham he'd smoked in his hollowed-out cypress stump. But Cy butchered only once a year. She wondered suddenly if Jess liked bacon.

So what if he did? a voice countered. He'd be around just two, maybe three weeks, to help with the chores until she could manage alone. Then he would be gone.

Caroline's nasal voice rose. "Why, of course she didn't!"

The six bonnets drew back like the unfolding petals of a daisy.

"But why not?" someone ventured.

"It just isn't done, Millie. My goodness, you'd think you never…"

The low buzzing of ladies' voices resumed, and Ellen devoured another bite of potato salad. Oh, it was heavenly to be part of this circle. To be accepted by the townspeople despite the behavior of her father when he was alive. And didn't the grass smell sweet today? And the pine trees…

She tipped her head up to feel the sun on her face, and spied Jess casually leaning against a tree, watching a game of horseshoes. A ringer clanged, and he looked up, catching her gaze across the wide expanse of lawn. Without altering his stance, he inclined his head. He didn't smile at her like the other men did. Jess wasn't a smiling sort of man. But he certainly looked his fill.

"…don't you think, Ellen?" Millie Shonski peered at her with narrowed brown eyes. "Ellen?"

Ellen wrenched her attention back to the ladies' circle, aware of an insistent, hungry clenching in her lower belly. Probably too much potato salad.

Or maybe too much Jess Flint.

"What, Millie?" She tried to look attentive while the mayor's wife repeated the question.

"Who is that man over there? The one who brought you into town?"

"His name is Jess Flint. He's the man I hired to help me when I broke my leg."

"Mighty good-looking fellow," someone remarked. "Don't you think so?"

"I hadn't noticed," Ellen lied.

"You hear anything from Dan?" Caroline inquired.

"Not yet, no."

"You still waiting for him to come back?" The acid in Caroline's voice pushed Ellen's good manners to the back burner.

"Of course I am. He is my husband, remember?"

"We remember," Millie said softly. "But it looks like *he* doesn't. It must be awful hard, Ellen."

Ellen thought about lying again, but the need to talk with real people about real things—her absent husband, her broken leg bone, even her rickety chicken house— drove her to honesty. Maybe too much honesty, because what she said next brought a stunned silence.

"What was hard at first was the worry," she blurted. "Was he alive? Why did he go away? After that it was hard keeping up the farm, planting and harvesting by myself." She paused and raised her chin. "Now what is hard is being so lonely I ache at night."

In the ensuing quiet Ellen focused on a pair of chattering sparrows in the oak branches above her head. She heard the clang of horseshoes from the pit, the quick roar of men's jubilant voices and the ragged thrumming of her heart. *What had she said?*

The Presbyterian ladies sat in complete silence for the first time Ellen could ever remember. Ladies in polite society, even in a town the size of Willow Flat, did not mention their intimate feelings. She'd been lying for years, she realized. To the church ladies. To her friends and the kind neighbors who reached out to help her. To herself.

It was such a relief to be honest!

A fiddle began to tune up. Thank God, the dancing

would start and her inappropriate outburst would be forgotten. "Grab yer partners," a male voice bellowed. In a flutter of petticoats, the ladies rose, fussed their skirts into place and unpinned their hats.

The fiddler broke into a fast reel and the Presbyterian ladies' circle dissolved in the direction of the makeshift plank dance floor.

Ellen found she could not get up with her new cast weighing her down. She gritted her teeth against the sting of tears. *And that's another thing that is hard—doing everything by myself. Damn you, Dan! We promised for better or worse. Well, this is the worse part and you're not even here!*

When the fiddle music started, Jess ambled away from the horseshoe pit. Maybe he'd listen, pick up a new tune. What he should do was pray to God nobody recognized him.

Across the park he watched the billowing of skirts and patting of hairdos as the little group around Ellen broke up. But Ellen did not rise and follow her friends. Instead she remained on the grass, straight-backed, her neck rigid and her chin raised.

When he realized she couldn't get up, something inside squeezed until it hurt. In a few long strides he stood before her, offering his hand.

"Oh, go away!"

Her voice sounded funny. Watery. Jess crouched down so he could see her face.

Her eyes shone oddly, and her mouth pressed into a grim line.

"Hurting?"

"Yes," she snapped. "But not the way you think."

"Good fiddler. Want to watch the dancing?"

"No, I don't want to watch. I want to be part of things. I want to dance, and I can't."

Without a word Jess stood and lifted her onto her feet, slipping the crutch under her armpit. "Yes you can. C'mon."

She wobbled. "I couldn't possibly dance. I can barely walk."

"The way I look at it, when you dance, you don't do it alone. It takes two."

"And that means?"

She was getting her fight back. Good for her. Again his insides squeezed.

"What does that mean, it takes two?" she repeated.

Jess couldn't stop his grin at her impatience.

"Well, hell, Ellen. I guess you'll just have to wait and let me show you."

Chapter Eight

Jess watched a muscular young man with a shock of chocolate-brown hair and eyes to match bend toward Ellen. "Care to dance, Miss Ellen?"

"No, thank you, Tom. I've a broken leg."

"Well, if that don't beat all. How'd you do a thing like that?"

Her mouth opened to reply, but before she could get a word out, another, older man elbowed the younger one aside, asking the same question. "Care to dance?"

"Thank you, Sheriff, but I—"

"I asked her first!"

"Dally your tongue, Tom. This here conversation's between two adults." Tom walked off and the sheriff, a paunchy man in a gray Stetson, plunked himself down on the bench beside her.

Jess shook his head as the steady parade of men made their way to where Ellen sat at the edge of the dance floor. In that yellow dress she was the prettiest woman within a square mile of the park. No wonder she was flooded with offers.

She seemed to know everybody—little boys in junior-size overalls, bent old grandfathers with whiskers and pipes, young girls with beribboned pigtails. Some of the men stayed to talk for a few minutes; others wandered off to find partners elsewhere. The townsfolk liked her. Respected her. The mercantile owner had said it: "Miss Ellen's good people."

Jess swallowed a snort. Ellen O'Brian was much, much more than that. She was an extraordinary woman. A desirable woman. If she were available, half the men in Lane County would propose marriage within an hour. Here came another one, a cowhand by the look of him, maybe a foreman from the way he handled himself. This one didn't ask Ellen to dance, just tipped his hat and settled his bony frame on the other side of the bench from the sheriff.

Surreptitiously, Jess moved closer, straining to hear.

She called him by his Christian name, William. The fellow rolled a cigarette and scratched a match with his thumbnail. While he worked his smoke down to a butt, he talked to her. Jess could catch only a word here and there—well digging…alfalfa…Riverton…dog named Smoky…Sheriff DeWitt…jailbreak….

Every nerve in Jess's body went numb. Riverton? *Jailbreak?* He leaned closer.

"…three men…heading south." Oh, God.

The sheriff ambled off, and then the cowboy went to fetch Ellen some lemonade. Jess studied the back of her neck where her hair curled beneath the straw hat. He wanted to touch her there, wanted to… Before he knew what he was doing, he was standing in front of her.

"Ellen, you want to try dancing?"

She looked up, interest sparkling in her eyes. "Yes, I surely would. But how can I?"

"Easy. You let the foot on your broken leg side rest on the top of my boot. When I move that foot, I'll lift you just a little."

"I—I'd better not. William is bringing lemonade, and I should—"

"You should dance, Ellen. With me. Forget about the lemonade. And about William," he added under his breath.

He drew her up, slipped his arm around her waist and frog-walked her slowly onto the dance floor. With both hands at her waist, he steadied her on the smooth plank surface, stepped in close behind her and turned her to face him.

"Lift your arms."

"Jess, I—"

"I'll hold you. Lift your arms. Now, put your left hand on my shoulder."

With a little frown, she touched him lightly and he folded her right hand in his. The fiddle was playing a jig of some kind. Didn't matter. He and Ellen were going to do a two-step, very, very slowly. He waited until he felt her small shoe press the top of his boot, and then he took a step. She gasped and faltered, but he tightened his arm at her waist and slowly swung her forward.

"Jess, I can't!"

"Yes, you can. You want to, don't you?"

She clutched his shoulder. "Yes! Oh, I do want to, more than…even more than eating potato salad!"

"Well then, try." He took another step, pulling her with him, and she began to move. "Am I hurting you?"

"Not at all. I—it feels wonderful. Wonderful!" She smiled at him and his heart rolled in a slow somersault. Over her shoulder he watched William, a glass of lemonade in each hand, standing by the now-empty bench with a puzzled look on his narrow face.

Jess kept Ellen facing away from him. After a moment, William offered the extra glass to a plump, dark-haired woman in a purple dress. Jess sneaked a glance at Ellen, but her eyes were now hidden under her hat brim.

"Could you take that thing off? Brim's getting in the way."

"No, I cannot. Not without using both hands, and if I do that, I'll tip over."

"I'll do it, then."

"It's pinned at the back." She tipped her head down so he could see where, and the straw brim scratched against his nose.

He jerked his head back. "Watch out. You've got a lethal weapon there."

"You should see my hat pin!"

He located it, pulled it out with his thumb and fore-finger and stared at it. A six-inch stiletto if he'd ever seen one. "This is downright dangerous, you know that?"

"Of course I know it. Why do you think ladies wear hat pins?"

"I always thought it was to keep your hat from blowing off." He lifted the straw object from her head, and when they passed near the wooden bench on their slow circuit about the floor, he sent it sailing. It settled on the lap of the woman in the purple dress.

"That's Millie Shonski, the mayor's wife," Ellen whispered.

Her warm body moved under his fingers, which were splayed at her back. "Right now, I don't care who she is."

"You would if you knew how she loves tittle-tattle."

"No," Jess said. "I wouldn't." *Not when I'm dancing with you.*

The fiddle ended the jig with a flourish, then lapsed into a rhythm slow enough to match his and Ellen's steps.

"Easier now?" he murmured. His chin was so close to her hair he could feel its warmth, smell the fresh scent of her soap.

She nodded. "I'm keeping an eye on Millie."

"Don't," he admonished softly. "Keep your attention on me. My feet," he corrected. "So you won't lose your step."

She nodded, and her chin brushed his shoulder. He held her tight in his arms, felt a tiny gust of warm air near his ear. He turned his face into her hair and felt her stiffen.

"Don't, Ellen," he said. "Don't pull away."

"Millie is watching," she whispered.

He closed his eyes and spoke for the first time he could remember without weighing each word. "Stay. Stay right where you are. I haven't held a woman in my arms for ten years, and I don't give a damn about Millie Shonski."

"Jess, I think…"

"Don't think. Not now." He drank in her scent, her strength, the sweetness she didn't know she had. He held her, warm and alive, as close as he dared, felt her breasts brush his shirt front. Fire crawled into his chest, down his arms, into his groin. Fire like he'd never felt for any woman.

Ellen lifted her head, looked into his eyes, and at that moment he was lost. Yesterday all he'd wanted was the money, and to hell with her. Now he wanted to protect her with his last breath. He knew he was looking at life or death, and all he wanted was Ellen.

His breath choked off and for a full five seconds Jess thought he'd never draw another. He knew now that he had to tell her about himself, but not yet. Oh, God, not yet.

She'd know about the jailbreak. All at once he wanted everything to stop. He wanted, he realized with a knife slash into his gut, to keep Ellen from being hurt.

What was he thinking? *You want to protect her?* What the devil was happening to him?

His warm fingers tightened about hers, more than decorum allowed. But still not as much as Ellen wanted.

She didn't want to think about Millie Shonski, or about what was taking place. She just wanted to enjoy being alive after so many endless months of feeling dead inside.

She concentrated on moving her injured leg when he moved his. Their movements, their touching kindled the strangest sensation inside her, as if she had gulped down a pot of warm honey laced with stars. She felt hot and shaky in a way she never had until this moment. Not even with Dan.

She sucked in a gulp of the pine-scented air. She wouldn't think of Dan now, not with this new searing wind tearing at her insides. She would think only of this moment, being held in a man's arms, feeling treasured. Wanted.

"Ellen," he murmured. "There's something I have to tell you."

Her heart clenched. "What is it?"

"Not now. After this dance is over, let's ride back to the farm. We need to talk some."

The minute they rode past the last building on Willow Flat's main street and veered onto Creek Road, Ellen turned her face to his and voiced the question he'd been expecting for the last half hour. "Tell me what?"

His throat closed. She'd tied her hat ribbons around her throat so the hat hung at her back; now he watched it swing across her yellow dress with each motion of the horse.

When he told her, she'd have hornets in her bonnet for sure. He wanted their slow ride back to the farm to last awhile longer. A lot longer. He'd also like to see her smile at him tomorrow morning when he brought in the eggs.

Oh, hell. He'd known it couldn't last. His belly twisted. The minute he opened his mouth, it would all crumble.

The expression in her eyes wavered back and forth between curiosity and fear. "Tell me," she insisted.

Dammit to hell. He sure hadn't planned for the price to be so high.

"I guess you heard about the Riverton jailbreak."

"Yes. William Turner mentioned it. The Roper gang."

"Ryder," he corrected. "The Ryder gang."

She shot him a quick look. "William thought I should

know about it, since I'm alone on the farm. He thinks I should have a watchdog."

"I think so, too." *But it's too late,* a voice yammered. *Now it's cards-on-the-table time.*

"Perhaps I will get a dog later. Right now, I have a hired man." She looked straight into his eyes when she said it. When she didn't look away, he touched her shoulder with his free hand.

"Ellen, I'm not what you think. I'm not a hired man."

"You are at the moment. What else you may be I don't care to know."

"Sure wish it was that simple."

"And it isn't?" Her voice was soft, verging on shaky. This meant something to her, he realized. It was more than simple curiosity; she was afraid of what he had to tell her.

"No, it isn't simple. Listen, Ellen, William was right. You should know about the Riverton jailbreak. It will affect you."

"Why should it? Riverton is hundreds of miles from here. Besides, I don't know anyone in jai—" She sucked in her breath and her eyes went wide.

"Dan," she murmured. "He's been in jail all this time?" Her voice changed. "What has he done? Why didn't he write and tell me?"

"Probably didn't want you to know."

Her face went white. "But I'm his wife! That should mean something to him!"

"Yeah. It should."

She slanted a penetrating look at Jess, her blue eyes snapping with fury. "Just how do you know all this, about Dan being in jail? In the Riverton jail in particular? How?" She accompanied the last word with a sharp poke at his chest.

"I once rode with the Ryder gang."

She stared at him. "You what? I don't believe it. You're an outlaw? That's not possible." A frown pulled her dark eyebrows into a scowl. "*Are* you an outlaw?"

"I used to be."

"Exactly what does the Ryder gang do to get thrown in jail?"

"Rob trains."

The silence pressed around Ellen like a hot, sultry night. Jess Flint had robbed trains? *Dan* had robbed trains? Had been incarcerated! *Had escaped?*

"He'll be coming home," she said in a suddenly quavery voice. "Back to our farm."

"Most likely." Jess didn't say anything else for a long while.

Ellen struggled to absorb the words, but the buzzing inside her head kept the pieces of the puzzle floating just out of reach. How quickly her life had turned upside down. An hour ago…

Her cheeks grew hot. An hour ago she hadn't been thinking about Dan at all. She'd been thinking about Jess Flint.

An hour ago, she might have…what? Broken her wedding vows?

No, she could never do that. A promise was a promise.

"I know it's hard to stomach. I'm sorry I had to be the one to tell you."

She wanted to scream. "But you *didn't* tell me. You knew all along, and you didn't tell me until now!" Her voice rose in near hysteria, but she was so furious she didn't care. She hoped she would spook the horse and Jess would tumble off. She hoped she'd burst his eardrums.

"How *could* you?" she shouted in his face. "You lying skunk. You damn mean lying skunk! Let me off the horse this instant."

"Not yet, Ellen. There's…" he closed his eyes momentarily "…there's more."

Incredulous, she stared at him. "More? What 'more'?" She punched her balled up fist into his chest. "Tell me, you snake."

He caught her hand, imprisoned it in his. "Would it do any good if I said I was sorry?"

"No! It would do no good at all."

She tried to jerk out of his grasp, but he lifted his arms and pinned her against him. "Ellen. *Ellen.*"

She went perfectly still. "All right, tell me the rest, damn you. Get it over with."

Chapter Nine

Jess reached out and laid his hand on Ellen's hair, pressed her face into his shoulder. "All right, I'll tell you. It's kind of a long story, so bear with me." He looked at her hands, still fisted in her lap. Damn.

He closed his eyes momentarily. "After the war, and…after some other things, I felt pretty footloose. Had a big chip on my shoulder after being captured and held in that Richmond prison so long. Knew I'd die if I didn't get out. It was overcrowded, with even the officers jammed in like sardines. No sanitation. Damn little water and what moldy rations they served were inedible.

"Guess you could say I carried a grudge from the day I left Richmond, hidden in a broken-down carriage I stole from…never mind. Anyway, I headed out West and met up with an old…" He was about to say "friend," but changed his mind. "That's what I've got to tell you, Ellen. I rode with a gang of outlaws."

"You're not a stupid man, Jess. But that was a foolish thing to do, get mixed up with outlaws."

Jess shrugged. "I've done worse. But that's not the point."

Ellen tried to pull away, but he tightened an arm around her shoulders, preventing her movement.

"Go on." She put an edge in her voice.

"Dan…we called him Danny Boy…joined the gang about two years ago. Right about that time the boys pistol-whipped a train engineer. That didn't set too well with me, and then during the very next job one of the boys shot a man. Killed him. That night I pulled out."

Ellen listened in silence, her pale face impassive. "Did you ever kill anyone?"

"Not as an outlaw, no. I did kill a good number of men in the war."

"Did you get rich robbing trains?" Her voice crackled with anger.

"Nope. When I walked away, I left my share of the money behind."

She skewered him with a look so sharp it could cut glass. "Why did you come to my farm?"

His breath hitched in. After a long moment he blew it out in a long sigh. "I'll be honest with you, Ellen. I never liked Dan much."

"Oh? And why not?"

"He was young and cocky. Bragged a lot."

"About the farm?"

Jess would give anything if he could lie to her now. What he knew about Dan was that he wasn't one-tenth the man Ellen deserved.

"No, not about the farm. About a robbery he'd pulled

off alone, just before he joined up with us. He told us how he'd sneaked back to his farm and buried the take someplace on the property."

She went rigid. "He came back to the farm? And he didn't let me know?"

"That's what he said. He was always peacock-proud of getting away with it."

"Let me down, Jess. I'm going to be sick." ·

"No, you're not. You'll have a good cry and put a mad on for a few days, and then you'll get over your frothy spell and do what needs to be done."

"What in God's name makes you think so?" She spat the words at him, but her lips were beginning to tremble.

Jess shook his head. "Dunno, exactly. Just a feeling."

"Based on what?" she demanded.

He ignored the question. "There'll be three of them. Dan and two others. They'll be here in a few days, and we need to get ready."

"We?" Her eyes narrowed in sudden comprehension. "You came here to dig up that money for yourself."

"I did, yes."

"That puts us on opposite sides of the fence, mister. When Dan gets home he'll run you off. Or shoot you," she added with satisfaction.

"No, he won't, Ellen. He'll dig up the gold, split it three, maybe four ways, if I get lucky, and then he'll ride out. Away from you."

"He will do no such thing! I know him better than you do. He's not what you think."

Jess gave her a little shake. "He is exactly what I think. A gambler. A cheat."

"But he…he loves me." She was close to tears. Jess hated to push the matter, but she had to know the truth.

"He does love you, Ellen. He bragged all the time about his pretty wife. But he loves robbing trains more."

"I cannot believe that."

"It's true." Jess closed his eyes at the anguish he saw in hers. "Dammit, I hate telling you this more than I can say."

The horse reached the gate and tried to nose it open. Jess knew he should dismount and unlatch it, but with Ellen in his arms he didn't want to move.

"I hate you," she muttered.

"Thought you would," he said. "But I had to tell you anyway."

"You have destroyed what little I have left in life." Her voice was low and wobbly. "I will hate you for the rest of my days."

"Maybe so. But if you want your life to last till next Sunday, you'll do as I say."

Her eyes blazed fire. "Why should I? Give me one reason why I should listen to anything—*anything!*—you have to say."

Jess stepped the horse parallel to the gate and leaned down to unlatch it. "The reason is simple. Because you stand a better chance with me."

He walked the horse through the gate and relatched it.

"What does that mean, I stand a better chance with you? Why on earth should I trust you, of all people?"

He dismounted and led the horse toward the back porch, speaking to her over his shoulder. "First, I'm a better shot than Dan. Better than Gray, who'll be riding with him. Don't know about J.D."

"And? What's number two? Some crazy idea about—"

"Second," Jess interrupted, "I decided something this afternoon at the picnic, when I was watching you sitting under the oak tree with your lady friends. I decided I'm more interested in keeping you safe than I am in the gold. I've decided that I'll stand with you."

From the look on her face, he thought she either didn't hear him or didn't believe him. When he reached up to lift her off Tiny's back, she shrank away from him.

Ellen had no idea how she reached the kitchen, no memory of climbing the back steps and clunking across the wash porch, but she must have done so. Either that or Jess had carried her in, but her rage at him made her doubt that. She couldn't stand the thought of being anywhere near him, at least not until she calmed down some. Otherwise she might kill him.

And speaking of wanting to kill someone… *Dan had come to the farm and he didn't even want to see me? Speak to me?*

She lifted a plate from the stack on the shelf and hurled it onto the floor with a satisfying smash. Another, one with blue flowers around the rim, landed with a crash. None of her china matched anymore, so what did it matter?

And Jess! Goddam him to hell. She'd never hated someone with such venomous clarity, not even her drunken father. The hurt and fury she'd held inside her boiled up like a vat of hot, smelly tallow.

Her gaze fell on the curtained space underneath the sink where Dan's shotgun rested. She kicked the curtain aside with her crutch and saw the gleam of blue steel. She was bending toward the weapon, reaching out one hand before she caught herself.

No, she decided. She couldn't kill a man. It was wrong. Besides, if she did, she really would be alone. Helpless. And that would be foolish.

What if she just threatened him? Cocked the weapon so he could hear it, let him know she had him in her sights? The weasel had purposely deceived her. She wanted to see fear in his eyes. She wanted him to pay for what he'd done.

Why, *why* had Jess lied to her? And for Lord's sake, why had he said that he would stand with her? Her hired man was a skunk of the lowest order and a mystery as well. She would never understand him.

And what about Dan?

Dan was another mystery. She turned awkwardly back to the shelf for another plate, and this time she added a teacup and saucer, too. The clinkery sounds they made crashing onto the floor eased the knot in her belly. Odd, how much better that made her feel.

When she ran out of china to smash she knew she would begin to cry. Already her throat ached. Letting the anguish out would help, but, well, she wasn't finished being mad.

And hurt.

And…puzzled.

She flung the empty teakettle onto the back porch, smiling as she heard the metal utensil tumble across the floor and lodge against the screen door. She was being childish, she knew. At the moment she didn't care. She heaved the iron frying pan after it and then went back to her plates. She would break all but one. And she would never, *never* take in a hungry cowboy again.

Three soup bowls crashed into the iron stove, one after the other. She had never allowed herself a fit of temper all the time she was growing up. Hadn't allowed herself to disturb her father out of fear of what he would do to her. Or to Mama, before she died, anyway. Too many times Ellen had hidden in the attic to avoid a beating; when Pa was drunk he couldn't manage to climb the steep steps up to her hiding place.

She hurled another bowl at the wall. She'd have to sweep it all up later, she thought dimly. But it was worth it. Being deliberately destructive seemed to ease the sick, tight feeling in her belly.

Purposely setting rational thought aside, she smashed two more plates and a gold-rimmed vegetable bowl against the kitchen table. Her arms were getting tired. By now, she had to heave so hard to break the china, it took three tries.

In a daze she stared down at the shards sprayed over the table, the floor, the stove. Enough.

Just one more thing. Clenching her teeth, she dragged herself over to the condiments shelf, raked the bottle of port off the top and heaved it into the sink as hard as she could. It split open with a satisfying clunk, and that was what finally brought her back to reason.

The pain she'd been avoiding sliced into her shaking body like the jagged teeth of a crosscut saw. She opened her mouth and screamed. Shouted words she hadn't realized she knew until she heard her hoarse voice yelling them. Then tears, hot and bitter, gushed forth. A crushing heaviness pressed on her breastbone, radiated into her throat until she could no longer utter a sound.

She wept. Over the next hour of choking sobs the hurt slowly subsided into a small, hard knot in her belly. Her eyes felt hot and swollen. When she had no more tears in her, she blew her nose on her pocket handkerchief, stuffed it into her waistband and dragged her aching body up the stairs to bed.

Jess leaned against the open barn door, listening to the noises coming from the house. The sound of breaking china carried in the warm night air, loud enough to unsettle the chickens. Loud enough to drive iron spikes into his gut.

More crashing sounds, then the thunk of something heavy on the back porch—a frying pan, maybe. Or the cake pans. Both, probably. The way she was going, she'd destroy the whole kitchen before morning. Well, he guessed she had plenty to be riled up about.

Or she might turn her anger against herself. He knew about that; you gained nothing and got hurt in the process. He pictured her upstairs in her bedroom, gulping mouthfuls of wine from the wedding gift bottle of port.

A wail of agony broke the brief stillness, then screams of rage and pain. His throat grew hot and tight as he listened to the sounds. At this moment he wished he'd never laid eyes on Ellen O'Brian. Never conceived the idea of one-upping that bastard Dan for cheating him.

She sobbed for what seemed an hour, maybe two, and then the glow of a lantern flickered, disappeared, and reappeared in her bedroom window.

The tiny crack that had nibbled into Jess's heart widened with a jolt. He'd planned to dig up the stash Danny Boy bragged about, take his cut from the train jobs and ride out. He hadn't planned on Ellen.

And she sure as hell hadn't planned on confronting husband Dan's real priorities. Hadn't a way in hell to survive what Jess knew was coming. Hell, he should have shot the cheating Irish scum when he had the chance.

He figured he and Ellen had three days at the most before the lid blew off. He shifted restlessly against the splintery barn door and began making his plan.

Jess stayed clear of Ellen for the first half of the following day. Before she came downstairs for breakfast he swept up the shards of china and replaced the teakettle and the frying pan on the stove. The sink reeked of port. He lifted out the crimson-stained pieces of glass, wondering if she'd drunk any before she smashed the bottle.

Deciding he'd kill two birds with one stone by burying the refuse in the next five-square-foot section to be searched, he tramped out to the apple orchard and began digging, deeper and wider than necessary.

He was bending over the shovel when he heard irregular steps at his back. Ellen stalked toward him in tight-lipped silence. Her face under the blue sunbonnet looked ravaged, her eyes puffy. A blade of agony bored into his breastbone.

She halted, fisted her free hand on her hip and

scowled at the gash he'd made in the earth. "Just what do you think you're doing?"

Jess wiped his sleeve across his forehead. "Trying to locate the gold Dan buried." He tried to meet her eyes, but she wouldn't look at him.

"I don't believe you."

"It's the truth, Ellen. If we can find it before Dan gets here, he won't have a reason to stay. He'll move on, and you'll be safe."

She shot him a withering look. "You mean *you* will be safe. Dan does have a reason to stay—the farm. Me. If 'we' find the money, you will be long gone before Dan comes."

"I'm not fool enough to ask you to trust me. Especially now that—"

"I certainly do not trust you. I never should have in the first place, and I never will again."

"Yeah, you said as much last night. I won't argue that I came here with a selfish intent. But unless you want to hightail it into town for a week, you're stuck with me. I'm the only help you've got."

"I will never abandon this farm, not even for a week."

Jess exhaled a sigh. "I figured you'd feel that way. If I can't convince you of some basic facts, guess I won't be able to talk you into vacating the place for your own safety."

"You've got that right, mister."

For a woman crushed with grief, she sure had a sharp edge in her voice. Like a raspy grinder.

"Besides," she snapped, "Dan is no threat to me. It's you he'll shoot on sight. Maybe I will even suggest it to him."

"For the last time, Ellen, I'm asking you to leave.

Please. Take Tiny and go on into town. Stay with your uncle, the doctor."

Jess watched her lips press together so hard they looked bloodless. "I am staying right here. My vegetables need weeding."

Something inside Jess snapped. "Then help me search, dammit. I've made a map of your property and marked off sections. I've done eight, got thirteen more to go over. You stay, you help me."

"I don't take orders from you!"

That did it. He dropped the shovel and tramped heavily to where she stood. "Lady, you want to live through this, you'll damn well do as I say." He laid both hands on her shoulders and gave her a rough shake. "You savvy?"

"Take your hands off me!"

Jess lifted his arms and dropped them to his sides, but he didn't step back. "I said, do you savvy?" he shouted.

A tremor crossed her face, but she didn't move. She stood gazing at him a long, long time, her eyes so cold and hard they looked like polished stones. "Yes," she hissed at last. "I savvy. More than you think."

"Time's running out, Ellen. With both of us looking for the gold, we'll have a better chance."

Again she just stared at him, but her eyes changed. In their depths he saw pain and resignation. She might look womanly on the outside, but on the inside she was tough as whang leather.

She had intelligence and she had courage.

Together, maybe they'd have a fighting chance.

Chapter Ten

The instant Doc turned the corner onto Chestnut Lane, he felt his pulse rate jump. He worked to keep his feet moving at the same steady pace, forced himself to breathe in the tree-scented morning air. His shoes crunched over the leaf-littered path approaching the rambling structure Iona had turned into a boarding-house after pneumonia had taken her husband eight years before.

Every morning since, Doc walked the same route to his office. He took a different way home when his day ended, because at that hour Iona was busy serving supper to her six boarders and did not appear on her porch.

Self-consciously he straightened his cravat and strode forward, anxious for his daily glimpse of the widow Everett. When he reached the corner of the neat white fence that enclosed her front garden, his breath quickened. Today he would do it. He would speak to her…oh! And raise his hat, of course, as any gentleman should.

He lifted his gaze to the wide front veranda and felt

his breakfast porridge suddenly float up, weightless in his stomach.

She wasn't there!

Never once in all these years had she not been rocking gently on her porch when he passed. Even in winter, when the icy wind stiffened his fingers and snow drifted from the chestnut branches, turning his nose and ears red, even on the coldest morning, there she would be, bundled to her chin in a fur wrap with a knitted wool fascinator about her head that almost obscured her delicate, heart-shaped face.

But not today. His heart hiccupped. His footsteps slowed by her front gate. Was she ill? Suddenly he couldn't draw a breath.

And then a movement beside her front steps caught his attention and he came to an abrupt stop. A slight figure in blue denim farmer's overalls and a ragged-looking red plaid shirt crouched over the front garden bed. A dainty hand pushed a trowel into the soil.

Doc froze, speechless. What was his darling Iona Everett doing on her hands and knees in the dirt? Wearing overalls! Never in his life had he seen his beautiful Iona in anything but pastel-colored dresses so sheer and ruffly they looked like spun sugar.

His hand shaking, he lifted his hat just as she turned in his direction. Her soft gray eyes went wide and then for some reason her hands flew to her hair, tied up under a blue bandanna.

Doc stood mesmerized, his hat still in his raised hand. *Speak to her!* he ordered. *Say something. Anything. Say good morning, just as if you didn't feel pole-axed every time you laid eyes on her.*

He opened lips that had gone strangely numb. "G—"

She cut him off. "Daffodils," she called. She gestured with her trowel toward a pile of brown lumps beside her. Then she sent him a smile that buckled his knees.

His feet began to move forward on their own accord. After a moment he resettled the hat on a head suddenly swelled with stars careening behind his eyes.

When he reached the end of her trim white fence, he risked a glance back at her. She was bending over, dropping something into the earth.

Daffodils. His beloved was planting bulbs for next spring. Doc thought he would melt with joy, watching her. She was a lot like his niece, Ellen; both women liked to grub around in garden dirt.

Next time, he vowed. Next time—tomorrow—he would manage to look at Iona and stammer out an entire word.

Working side by side without speaking, Ellen and Jess covered four sections on the hand-drawn map grid, methodically poking sharpened steel fence stakes into the earth at measured intervals. Each time the rod disappeared hilt-deep without hitting anything larger than a rock, Ellen's frustration mounted.

The midday heat seared her shoulders right through the faded print blouse. Dan's shirt would have provided better protection from the merciless sun, but this morning she couldn't bear to touch a single one of his garments.

"Nuthin'," Jess would mutter periodically. "Let's move on." They shifted to another marked-out area.

Her thoughts churned as she worked alongside him.

What would happen if they *did* find the stash? What would Jess do?

He will leave, of course. Take the money and skedaddle.

On second thought, maybe he wouldn't. At least not until Dan returned to help her with the farm. Then there would be nothing to prevent Jess from carrying out his original plan.

But he couldn't carry the gold on foot; he'd need a horse. Not Tiny. Her plow horse would be too slow. Maybe he planned to steal a mount from the Ryder gang when they arrived.

Her heart gave a little start. Good riddance to him, then! She hoped the gang would give chase and when they caught up to Jess they would…they would…string him up from the nearest tree.

Would Dan join in the chase? Or would he stay on the farm with her? At this point, she didn't trust either her so-called hired man *or* her husband.

Her perspiration-slicked hair straggled from under the sunbonnet; the damp strands felt hot and sticky on the back of her neck. Tonight she'd have to wash her hair. Ellen clamped her jaw tight. It was hard enough balancing herself to stab these probes into the earth; the ordeal of washing her hair while balancing on her crutch made her groan aloud.

Jess straightened. "Tired?"

"Hot," she retorted. "Disgusted."

Jess squinted at the sun. "In another hour we can work on the shady side of the barn."

"No. I'm sick of this whole business. I keep asking

myself why I am tramping around my garden poking holes between my squash plants. Another hour and my head will explode."

He surveyed her with steady, dark eyes. "Can't quit, Ellen. Not if we want to stay alive."

"You mean if *you* want to stay alive."

"No," he said in a low, even voice. "I mean *we*. You and me."

Ellen sniffed. "Dan isn't going to shoot me. He'll be aiming at you."

"Wouldn't be too sure if I was you. A man with a gun in his hand can be unpredictable."

Jess took the steel rod out of her sweaty hands, joined it with his own and jabbed them both into the earth. "You ever handle a revolver?"

"No. I fired Dan's shotgun once at a coyote sneaking around the chicken house. The gunpowder smell was awful and my shoulder hurt afterward."

"Revolver has a kick, too. Trick is to anticipate it."

"I have no interest in firing a revolver, thank you."

He took a step toward her and laid one hand on her shoulder. "I know you don't."

Ellen jerked away. His touch unsettled her. "So, that's the end of that."

Jess shook his head. "Not quite. I'm going to teach you to handle a revolver."

"I don't want—"

"Heard you the first time." He gripped her elbow hard enough to make her gasp. "Let's go. Around the far side of the barn."

"Wait just one min—"

"C'mon. You can rest while I get my gun and some ammunition." He propelled her along beside him and settled her on a tree stump shaded by the east wall of the weatherbeaten barn. "I'll just be a minute."

Ellen watched him stride off in his curious, uneven gait. She'd be damned if she would just sit here waiting for him. She made a listless attempt to stand up, then decided she was too wrung out at the moment to move a single step.

When he returned he held a heavy-looking revolver in one hand, a box of cartridges in the other. "First thing, you load it."

"I don't want to load it."

"Like this." He cracked open the loading gate, slid a bullet into the first chamber, skipped one and then loaded four more bullets and snapped the chamber closed. Immediately he reopened the barrel and ejected the bullets into Ellen's lap.

"You try it."

"Certainly not! I have no interest whatever in—"

Jess grabbed her hand, wrapped her fingers around the butt and held them in place. "You might not have interest, Ellen. But you've got necessity. Now do what I say and load this damn gun!"

Ellen tried to slip her fingers out from under his hand, but he tightened his grip. "Do it," he ordered. "Like I showed you." He lifted his hand off hers and waited.

With short jerky motions she cracked the barrel, jammed the bullets in and snapped it shut without a hitch. Then she swung the weapon in a half circle and aimed it at his belt buckle.

Jess looked from her set, angry face to the revolver wobbling in her hand. "You have to cock it first to fire it."

"How do I do that?" she said through clenched teeth.

"Reach your thumb up to the hammer." He leaned toward her and pointed. "Just pull it back. When you hear the click, you're ready to fire."

She did as he said. The click of the hammer made him look back to her face. Hell, she was still mad as a bee-stung colt.

"Okay, now you can shoot me." He reached to the wavering barrel and steadied it with a forefinger. "Might want to hold it straight, otherwise no telling what you'll hit. Maybe my chest. Maybe my gut." He slapped his free hand against his belt. "A bit lower, and you'll blow off my—"

"Where," she said with venom in her voice, "would I aim if I wanted to kill you?"

Jess reached out and lifted the barrel until it pointed at his chest. "Here. Aim dead center."

She stared at him for a long time, then with a small moan of frustration, she let the revolver sink onto her lap. Jess breathed an inaudible sigh of relief.

"It's harder than you think to kill a man. You can't stop to think, you have to concentrate."

"I was concentrating just fine. My wrist got tired."

Jess grinned down at her. "Thank the Lord. Thought for sure I was a dead man."

"You knew I wouldn't shoot you," she said in a weary voice. "I'm too tired and sad and confused and…"

"I sure as hell didn't know." He lifted the weapon off her lap and carefully released the hammer. "But before you *do* shoot someone, you need to learn to control your shot. Get up."

He helped her stand, positioned her facing the side fence, and laid the revolver into her palm. "See that sunflower by the post? Aim for that."

When she raised her arm, Jess stepped in close to correct her stance. "Ease your shoulders down. Don't tense up." He watched her tongue flick across her lower lip, and his body went still. God, he wanted to touch her.

Very carefully he lifted off her sunbonnet. "Now, look straight down the barrel at that sunflower."

She tipped her head and sighted. He noticed the wisps of dark hair escaping the loosening bun at her neck, the smooth, pale skin behind her ear. A flicker of awareness spread along the flesh of his inner arm, fleeting as a kiss.

Her extended arm began to tremble with the weight of the weapon.

"Your arm's not strong enough, Ellen. Use both hands." He lifted her left hand to curl around the gun butt over her right.

"I can't balance this way, Jess. I need one hand on my crutch."

"Find something to lean on, then. You need two hands." He moved closer, put his hands at her waist and drew her back against him. Under his fingers her body felt warm and soft. He smiled to himself. No corset.

"Now, when the gun fires, it'll kick back some. Your elbow will feel it most. Helps not to stand too stiff."

"I am not stiff," she snapped.

He stifled an urge to laugh. "You ready?"

"Ready." Her voice sounded tight as new barbwire.

"Okay," he murmured near her temple. "Take a breath."

She inhaled, pressing her spine subtly against his chest.

"Now let it out partway and squeeze the trigger."

The report of the gun tore through the lazy afternoon stillness. Ellen jerked and cried out. The sunflower still bobbed at the fence, but the chickens squawked and cackled as if a coyote had sneaked into one of their nests.

She moaned. "I didn't hit one of my hens, did I?"

Jess eyed the screened-off yard where the birds flapped their wings and skittered back and forth. "Nope. But just to be safe, I'm going to lock the cow in the barn."

Ten minutes later, with the chickens shut in the henhouse and Florence safe inside her stall, they resumed the lesson.

"How's your arm?" he asked when she raised the revolver again.

"Elbow tingles. Are my shoulders okay?"

"Relax them. Let them drop." He reached out to press them down, then rethought his intent. The less he touched her the better.

"I am shooting that sunflower, right?" She took careful aim and fired.

This time a voice yelped from the road. "Hold your fire!"

Ellen paid no attention. "I hit it! Look, Jess, the bullet went right through it. See the hole?"

"I see it. Reload, Ellen. I'd guess our lesson's not quite over yet."

Jess slipped his other Colt from his belt and aimed it in the direction of the voice, but Ellen placed a restraining hand on his arm. Her touch sent a jolt of heat straight into his chest.

"Don't shoot, Jess. It's William." She laid the revolver she'd just fired onto the stump behind her and started for the front fence. The cowbell Jess had rigged up as a warning system clanked loudly as the gate swung open. At the unexpected noise, Ellen threw him a sour look.

The young brown-eyed man Jess had seen at the Sunday picnic walked a dun mare into the yard, dismounted and looped the reins over the gate post just as Ellen approached. A dog trotted after him.

"Why, William, I did not expect a visit from you today."

"Miss Ellen." He tipped a new-looking tan Stetson and then turned to Jess. "Mr. Flint."

Jess gave him an almost imperceptible nod and shifted his gaze back to Ellen.

"'S not really a social call, Miss Ellen. They handed out the ribbons for the cakes after you left, so I brought yours. Seems you won first place." He dug a lopsided blue ribbon bow out of his vest pocket and pressed it into her hand. "Congratulations. Sure was good."

"Thank you, William." She half turned toward Jess and held out the prize while a slight smile curved her lips. "Mr. Flint deserves this as much as I do," she murmured.

William's brown eyebrows quirked, but he said nothing. Instead, he eyed the Colt in Jess's hand.

"Target practice," Jess said. "Sorry if I spooked your horse."

"N-no, you didn't. My dog, though, Shep's his name. He doesn't like gunfire."

Jess shoved the revolver back under his belt. "Smart dog."

"Would you stay for coffee?" Ellen said quickly.

"Not today. I just rode out to bring the ribbon and…" He hesitated, closed his mouth and then opened it.

"And?" Ellen prompted.

"I want you to keep Shep out here with you." The young man's eyes rested briefly on Jess, then returned to Ellen. "For, you know, for…protection."

"That is very thoughtful of you, William, but I am managing quite capably. So I couldn't possibly—"

"Thanks, Turner," Jess interrupted. "We'll feed him good."

William's expression moved from a grin into a frown. "Miss Ellen, could I speak to you in private?"

"Why, of course. Come on into the parlor."

Jess spun away toward the barn before she finished the sentence. "C'mon, Shep. I'll find you an old boot you can chew on." He strode away, the dog frisking at his heels.

William stared after the animal. "Well I'll be. Shep likes the ladies, but he doesn't usually take to men. Not right off at least." His gaze followed Jess until he disappeared into the barn. "Who is this man Flint, anyway?"

"He is…" Ellen swallowed, in a quandary as to what to say. Jess was an outlaw. At least he had been once. Sometimes he was appealingly human, and warm, even funny. Other times he was bossy as a schoolmaster. And now he was the man who had lied to her. And more.

"Mr. Flint is my hired man."

"Dan's not gonna like that one bit."

"Dan is not here," Ellen countered. "Mr. Flint is."

"Shucks, I can see that. If you needed help you could have come to me. I'll always do what I can for you, Miss Ellen. You know that."

Ellen nodded. She did know that. The devil of it was it didn't matter. William was sweet, a nice, reliable young man, but he didn't matter to her. Dan mattered.

Jess mattered.

"You reckon he's peeking at us from the loft window?"

Ellen laughed and patted William's arm. "Probably. He keeps an eye on me because that's what I pay him for." The small lie almost caught in her throat. She had no intention of paying Jess for his help. Not now. He seemed content with three meals a day and a bed in the hayloft, but that couldn't last. The minute he dug up Dan's cache of stolen money, Jess would leave her high and dry.

William scuffed his boot in the dirt. "Heck, I can feel his eyes diggin' into my back this very minute."

"Nonsense." But she couldn't help sneaking a look at the loft. It would be just like Jess to spy on them. But why should he? William was a friend, not a threat.

Jess stood to one side of the dusty window in the barn loft, absently scratching Shep's ear as he watched Ellen and young Turner in the barnyard below. Turner leaned forward and said something to her, and when she reached out and patted his arm, Jess clenched his fingers into a knot. With his other hand he smoothed the shiny steel barrel of his Colt. He hadn't shot a man since the war, but if Turner so much as laid a finger on her…

At his feet, Shep gave a tentative growl and gazed up at Jess with liquid brown eyes.

"Guess you're right, boy. Ellen can take care of herself with that young pup. Better save my bullets."

But he didn't holster his weapon until the dun-colored mare stepped through the gate and out onto the town road.

"What do you mean, jealous?" he muttered to the dog. "Never been jealous a day in my life and I'm not going to start now."

He pivoted away from the window. "C'mon, Shep. You need something to chew on." He climbed down the loft ladder and began rummaging in the tack room for one of Dan's old work boots.

Chapter Eleven

They ate supper at the kitchen table in strained silence, Jess forking down tomatoes with slow, purposeful motions, his eyes carefully expressionless, until Ellen couldn't stand it another minute.

"Say something!" she exclaimed abruptly.

His hand paused midway to his mouth. "Thought you hated it when I said something. Can't have it both ways." He refilled his fork and closed his lips over a slice of ripe tomato.

Ellen watched him chew and then swallow without looking at her. "I'd rather have conversation. Otherwise it's just like eating by myself."

But it isn't, a voice nagged. Just being in the same room with Jess, whether he talked or not, made her feel…different. As if something was weaving a connection between them. Something she couldn't see or measure, but *something.* When she was near him, searching the yard for Dan's treasure or sitting across from him at the kitchen table, her insides tumbled like laundry scrubbed on a tin washboard.

What complete and utter nonsense! The *something* between them was nothing more than pure anger and distrust. Still, when he looked across the table at her, as he was doing now, her blood raced through her veins and her body hummed as if invaded by a cloud of bees.

Jess laid his fork onto the plate before him. "Conversation, huh? Even if you don't want to hear what I say?"

Ellen blinked at the sound of his voice but managed to look him in the eye. "You could not possibly shock me more than you already have."

"Okay, here goes." His lips quirked in a lopsided smile. "You ever thought about getting your cow bred?"

Her coffee cup clunked onto the table. "What?"

"If Florence had a calf come spring, you could slaughter it in the fall, then you'd have meat for next winter."

Ellen stared at him. Calf? Whether her cow would calve in the spring was an odd concern for an outlaw intent on his own nefarious business.

He tipped his head down so she couldn't see his eyes. "Did I say something wrong?" Then he added, "Again?"

"Why on earth are you thinking about my cow?"

Methodically he sectioned a tomato into four quarters. "I wasn't. I was thinking about you."

The buzzing in her head grew stronger. "What about me?"

Purposefully he downed all four pieces of tomato, one by one, while Ellen waited.

"About whether you'll have meat this winter. About whether you should sink a well in case the creek goes

dry. About…whether you're ready for another surprise."
He went on eating in his slow, deliberate way, but he
looked like he was trying not to smile.

Ellen narrowed her eyes. "What kind of surprise?"

"How about I show you on the front porch, where it's
cooler. You go on out and sit in the rocker. I'll wash up
the plates and bring out the surprise."

"Is it a cake? You baked a cake by yourself?"

He shook his head. "We worked together all day.
When did I have a spare hour to mix up a cake?"

She couldn't help the smile that tugged at her own
mouth. "I thought maybe that blue ribbon went to
your head."

"Matter of fact, it did. Soon as we find Dan's mon—"

Ellen clattered to her feet and jammed the crutch
under her arm. "No more talk about Dan," she snapped.
"Or that money."

Jess lifted both arms as if to ward off a blow, but
Ellen just sniffed and plodded past him into the parlor
and out onto the front porch.

A breeze had come up. The air felt silky and smelled
of honeysuckle, and she settled into the wicker rocker
with a sigh of pleasure. Shep flopped down at her feet
and laid his black head across his paws. The setting sun
colored the sky crimson and purple, and she gazed out
across the valley where the wind rippled Cy Gundersen's
wheat field. It was so beautiful her throat tightened and
the hollow under her breastbone blossomed into an ache.

What surprise could Jess have? "I thought I'd heard
all of it," she muttered. But she guessed with a man like
Jess you'd never hear all of it. There would always be

something more hidden behind those determined, assessing eyes.

Her skin prickled. When she wasn't so mad at him she could spit, she wondered about him. Sometimes he had the wary look of a hunted animal. Sometimes he looked like the hunter. Tonight, she noted as he stepped out onto the porch, he looked like both hunter and hunted.

Her curiosity built until she couldn't hold back the question. "What is the surprise?"

"Here." He handed her a plate.

"An orange!" she breathed, staring at the succulent looking sections. "Wherever did you find an orange?"

Jess lowered himself onto the top step, stretching his long legs out in front of him. In his hand he held another orange, this one with the bright, pebbled skin still intact.

"Two oranges!" She slipped a segment into her mouth and bit into it. The rich, sweet flavor flooded the inside of her cheeks. She closed her eyes to savor the juice as it spurted over her tongue and slid down her throat. What heaven!

Without moving, she popped in another section, then smelled the sharp scent of orange peel. She looked down to see Jess sink his teeth into the navel end of the unpeeled fruit, dig his fingernails under the skin and slowly, methodically, strip the covering away from the ripe flesh underneath. His hands were gentle, his motions almost lazy as he worked. Handled that way, the orange looked as if it were being ravished before her eyes.

Her face burned. She shouldn't think such things!

But his hands… Merciful heavens, watching his hands made her feel strange inside. Hot and trembly, like a mare that's been ridden too hard.

She swallowed. "Did you steal them?"

"I bought them at the mercantile, the day I was in town." He spoke without looking up. "Thought you'd like them."

"I do. But oranges are a luxury I usually forgo."

"That's what Svensen said. He said you needed them."

"Needed them? What on earth did he mean?"

Jess ducked his head, concentrating on the fruit in his hands. "Well, to be honest with you, *Svensen* didn't exactly say that. I did."

A hot knife sliced into Ellen's chest. "How would you know what I needed?"

"Pretty obvious. You work too hard. Got to take time to enjoy more things."

"That is the very same lecture I get from Gabriel Svensen every single time I buy supplies."

"It's true, Ellen. You're wasting your life out here, holding on to the place for Dan." Jess spoke without raising his head. "Besides, I wanted to use those oranges to buy my way into your good graces."

"Bought with *my* money."

"With your money, yes. Seemed like a good idea." He stuffed a piece of fruit into his mouth, chewed appreciatively and swallowed, then twisted toward her and draped one wrist over his raised knees. "Damn good idea, don't you think?"

A flock of quivering hummingbirds sailed into her belly. Whenever he looked at her with those riveting purple-blue eyes, or worse, when he smiled at her, she felt all upside down. Light-headed.

And *that* was beyond the pale. She was a married woman! A respectable married woman did not dally with another man.

"Ellen, what is William Turner to you?"

She blinked at the question but was too tired to challenge it. "We grew up together here in Willow Flat. Went to school together. He…stood up for me against my father."

"He's in love with you." Jess said it in such a matter-of-fact tone Ellen wasn't sure she'd heard correctly.

"Surely you are joking?"

"Nope. You have feelings for him?"

"Of course I do. We have been friends for more than twenty years. I am very fond of William."

Jess grunted.

"I have, however, no feelings for William beyond friendship."

He grunted again.

"I love my husband."

"You do." It wasn't a question. Jess didn't intend it to be. "Even after what he's done? After leaving you alone out here for almost three years?"

"Of course I—" She snapped her mouth shut and Jess could see her mind working, turning over her feelings as she thought about Dan. He didn't understand exactly why he'd pushed the question at her, just that he wanted to know. Needed to know. In fact, dammit, it mattered to him more than it should.

"My father drank," she said in a flat tone. "And when

he drank he was violent. My mother died after one of his beatings, bearing a child he'd forced on her. The baby died as well." She stopped, swallowing audibly. "I married Dan to get away from him."

"Then what?" Jess kept his voice low.

"When Pa died, I used what inheritance he left me to make the down payment on this farm." She fell silent for a long minute. "But I was genuinely fond of Dan. I mean, I still am. Dan was handsome and charming and…and he protected me."

"And that's what loving a man is," Jess said dryly. Again, it wasn't a question.

Ellen blew out a shaky breath. "I think that love is sometimes very hard to recognize. It's something that is very rare between people."

Jess ate the rest of his orange in silence. "Pretty night," he said after a time. "Reminds me of home."

"North or south?"

"Beg pardon?"

"Union or Confederate? Where you grew up."

"Virginia. I fought under General Grant. I really admired Bobby Lee, though. Everybody did, Federal or Reb. His men thought he walked on water."

"That," Ellen said softly, "is a kind of love. It makes me cry when I think of it."

"That's loyalty, not love."

"Loyalty and love go hand in hand." She finished the last segment of her orange and set the plate on the floor, where Shep licked at it halfheartedly and went back to sleep. "You're sidestepping around something, Jess. What is it you want to know?"

"Don't know, exactly." He stood and leaned against the porch post, facing her. "You ever want something so much it hurts?"

"Yes. I want this farm. I want Dan to come home. And yet…" She dropped her face into her hands. "At the same time, I don't want you to leave."

Jess straightened and stared at her bent head. Her bun was coming loose again; dark brown curls brushed her neck. "I've waited days for you to say that."

"I don't understand myself anymore. Ever since I broke my leg, all sorts of wild and foolish things run through my mind."

"It's got nothing to do with your leg."

"Of course it does. It all started then, when I became completely helpless for the first time in my life. Dependent on you. I don't like it."

"Last time we talked, you said you hated my guts."

Her eyes blazed. "Maybe I still do!" she declared.

He took a step toward her. "I don't think so, Ellen."

She raised her chin. "No, you're right. I don't hate you. But I don't trust you. I don't think I even like you very much."

Jess advanced another step and she fluffed up in the rocker like a little banty rooster. "I think you're lying to me. Maybe to yourself as well."

Ellen tipped the rocker back as far as it would go to evade him. "Lying about what?"

"About how you really feel."

"About what? Dan? You?"

"All of it." Jess reached down, placed his hands under her shoulders and lifted her to stand in front of him.

"What are you doing?"

"Something I'll probably regret come morning." Slowly he moved his hands to her upper arms and held her still. Under his fingers her body trembled.

She took in a quick gasp of air and looked up into his eyes. "Probably? Why probably?"

"Because." He stepped into her warmth and pulled her close. "Because I don't have the right."

Her breath smelled of oranges.

"No," she murmured, her mouth mere inches from his. "You don't."

Chapter Twelve

Jess hesitated a moment, then caught Ellen's mouth under his. His lips were firm and warm, and after another hesitation he deepened the pressure and began to move his mouth over hers. Ellen couldn't think, couldn't breathe until he broke the kiss and whispered against her lips.

"I've wanted to do that ever since I walked in your gate."

"You shouldn't."

"I know that." He kissed her again. Reason fled in the wash of sweet, drowsy sensation that spread through her body. She wanted his mouth on hers, wanted to feel his arms around her, his hands on her skin.

Dear heaven, what was happening to her?

"Jess. Jess, please."

He lifted his head, breathing unevenly. "Tell me you don't want this, Ellen. Tell me, and I'll stop."

She opened her lips to reply and found she couldn't speak. The word *stop* lodged somewhere in her throat and she swallowed it back. She couldn't say it, because it wasn't true. She didn't want him to stop.

His warm breath gusted against her temple. "Tell me," he murmured.

Ellen closed her eyes and leaned into him, felt her breasts brush against his hard chest. "I can't."

His lips touched her cheek, dropped to her throat while his hands moved over her back and shoulders, restless and hungry. She tipped her head up, saw his face twisted with indecision, his eyes black with desire and something else. Pain.

"We have no right to this, Jess."

"I know. Never figured I did, just wanted it so bad, so deep, I couldn't let myself think about the rightness of it."

"We *must* think. *I* must. It is wrong, Jess."

"Sure doesn't feel like it," he said against her mouth.

No, it certainly did not. It felt wonderful. It should not feel wonderful, but it did. His hard, muscular body pressed to hers, his mouth, tender and demanding—none of it should feel right.

But it did. Oh, dear God, it did.

The realization whipped the blood in her veins to a hot, desperate longing. All she wanted at this moment was his mouth on hers. It terrified her.

It thrilled her.

She broke away from him. "I cannot do this, Jess. I owe my husband fidelity."

He nodded and stepped away from her, breathing hard. He held her gaze as he groped for her crutch, steadied her with a hand at her back while he fitted it under her arm. "If you want—"

"No," she said quickly. "I don't trust myself."

Jess chuckled low in his throat. "Ten minutes ago you didn't trust *me.* Maybe the wind's shifting."

"No, it is not. I still don't— Oh, I don't know what I think. My brain is all mixed up."

"Sounds like progress to me." She could tell he was grinning by the sound of his voice.

"Progress? Toward what? Dan will be here soon, and my life will pick up where it left off. You will leave. Dan will stay."

And she would be happy. If it was the last thing she ever did in her mortal life, she would be happy. She had earned it.

She clumped past him, avoiding his eyes. "Good night, Jess."

"Ellen." It was the only word he spoke, but her name on his lips sent a glow of warmth into her midsection. She kept moving, through the parlor and up the stairs one laborious step at a time.

Jess's gaze followed her until her slight form melted into the shadows on the landing. For one crazy minute he considered going after her, but instantly he realized he couldn't. He wouldn't, even if he could. Not yet. Not until she asked.

And he knew right down to his boots she would never do that. She'd wait for that bastard of a husband and go on wasting her youth making excuses for him. That was the problem with a good woman: she didn't take sin lightly.

"Shep, old boy." He bent to scratch the one tan ear, then moved to the black one. Part cattle or maybe sheepdog, probably. His quick, intelligent eyes missed nothing. Good watchdog. "Shep, how about you and me makin' a plan?"

Jess settled himself once more on the top step and snapped his fingers. The dog trotted over, licked at his hand with a wet, warm tongue and curled up at his side.

"Got to decide on some good hiding places, boy. Any suggestions?"

He considered the barn loft. Too obvious. The cow stall might work, especially if Florence was in there as well. Then again, he didn't want to risk getting Ellen's only milk cow killed by a stray bullet.

He thought for another ten minutes, then shook his head. "C'mon, Shep. Let's walk the place again, see what we can find."

The dog trotted down the steps after him, his claws clicking on the wood. The chicken house, maybe? The high branches of the pepper tree in the side yard? Nope. Ellen couldn't climb.

Over the next hour Jess tramped the entire farm from the front gate to the spindly apple orchard at the back of the property, from the clothesline to the cornfield across the creek.

The cornfield, that was it. The green stalks were taller than a man. If she made it to the cornfield, she could crawl to safety in the center.

His lips thinned. As a last resort, he would protect Ellen's body with his own.

"Try again, Ellen. Aim a little lower at first, then bring the barrel up slow."

Ellen groaned. She had to do it; Jess wouldn't let her

quit until he was certain she could hit something smaller than the henhouse. Her targeted sunflower bobbed insultingly in the breeze as if mocking her. The bullet hole she'd made through the yellow flower yesterday stared back at her like a small black eye.

She lifted the revolver again, then lowered it when her arm started to shake.

"You're tired," Jess said. "Try hanging your hand down at your side and flexing your fingers."

She was hot and sticky and hungry and miserable. Even her clenched teeth were hot. All morning they had spent probing the ground and digging holes in one marked-out section after another. Ever since noon and their lunch of bread and cheese, she had been target practicing.

So numb with fatigue she hadn't the energy to argue, she did as he directed, re-aimed and squeezed the trigger.

Another dark round eye stared back at her from the sunflower.

"Look what I did, Jess! I hit it exactly where I wanted. Exactly!" she squealed. "I bet even *you* couldn't do better."

He took the Colt from her hand, cracked open the barrel and reloaded all five chambers. Almost casually he raised the weapon and sighted down the barrel. "What are you willing to bet?"

"Why, I don't know. A cake?"

"And a kiss." He didn't look at her, just squeezed the trigger five times in rapid succession. A semicircle of small bullet holes etched a smile on the face of the sunflower.

Ellen removed her hands from her ears and stared at the line of black dots. Before her eyes, the flower head flopped over.

"I had no idea you could shoot like that."

"That makes us even," he said with a soft laugh. "I had no idea you could kiss like that."

Ellen clapped her hands to her burning cheeks. "I cannot imagine what you mean." She put as much ice in her voice as she could manage.

Without speaking, Jess ejected the spent shells and moved toward her. She backed away as fast as she could maneuver her crutch. "You wouldn't dare."

Jess grinned at her. "Not now, I wouldn't. After supper."

She was so nervous during supper she burned the butter beans and forgot the coffee. She told herself it couldn't be because of what Jess had said this afternoon, about winning a kiss. That wouldn't bother her one bit. She felt unsettled because…because Dan would be coming home. Returning to a woman who…who couldn't stop thinking about someone else.

Jess finished his cornbread and pushed his chair away from the table. "Forget the coffee. We need to talk."

"Talk! You want to talk? Not…not claim your kiss?" She meant to say "cake," but baking was the furthest thing from her mind.

"Later." He unfolded his limbs and stood up. "You feel up to walking some?"

"Now?"

"Not dark yet. Can you make it as far as the creek? Something I need to show you."

Ellen hesitated, one hand on the apron tie at her back. "What is it?"

"Just trust me, Ellen."

She huffed out a gust of air. "Don't be a fool. You know I don't trust you."

Jess looked straight into her eyes. "Yeah, I know. Come with me anyway."

Ellen's heart thumped and skittered. Why should she? *Because he is trying to help you.*

And why would he do that?

Because he doesn't want you to get hurt.

But that was unnecessary. Dan would take care of her when he came home. It was not Dan who was to be feared. It was Jess.

He moved to the back door and held the screen open for her. "I'm waiting."

Ellen yanked at the bow and jerked off her apron. It was no good trying to dissuade him. Once he made a decision about something, he was like the Rock of Gibraltar. If he had set his mind on that kiss she owed him, why not claim it right here and now?

A frown creased his forehead as he stood waiting for her. "You dithering or coming?"

"I do not dither."

"True enough." He walked beside her without saying another word, steering her to the barn. The place smelled of musty hay and horse droppings.

"C'mon." He pushed her into the tack room in the far corner. He'd straightened it up, she noted. Ropes and bridles dangled from nails newly pounded into the walls. A saddle rested on the battered desk Dan had used as a catchall for liniment and old towels. The desk, its top cleared of debris for the first time in years, had been shoved from the far wall to partially block the doorway. Brown grocer's paper had been tacked over the single window.

"All you'd have to do is use your backside and push the desk over a bit to stop the door. Then crawl under the knee space."

"Why on earth would I want to do that?"

Jess shot her a measuring glance, then licked his lips. "The window's covered, so nobody can see in. You might need a safe place to hide."

"From my own husband? Don't be ridiculous!"

He gripped her shoulders so hard she could feel all ten individual fingers. "Listen to me, Ellen. You haven't seen Dan in over two years. Could be he's not the same as you remember. Besides that, the two riding with him, Gray and J.D., are hotheaded and rough around the edges. And more."

"What 'more'? I hate it when you tell me only part of something."

His mouth narrowed into a grim line. "Gray is young. Headstrong. He shoots before he thinks. And J.D.…" Jess closed his eyes for a brief moment. "J.D. likes women."

Ellen sniffed. "Most men like women. What's wrong with that?"

Jess hesitated. "J.D. likes to hurt women. He likes to hear them scream."

Cold fear curled up Ellen's spine. "Those men are coming here? Why would Dan bring—?"

"Goddammit, Ellen, do I have to spell it out? Dan

rides with the gang. Since I pulled out, I hear they do more than rob trains."

She stiffened, staring fixedly at the top button on Jess's blue shirt. "It isn't true. Not the part about Dan."

"Suit yourself as to the truth of it. In a day or so you'll see for yourself. I'm just telling you what we're up against."

"I see." Her voice was chilly, but she couldn't help it. Part of it was anger at Jess's slur on her husband's character. Part of it was fear that he was telling her the truth.

He lifted his hands from her shoulders. "I want to show you another place you'd be safe."

"Really," she said with steel in her tone. She couldn't explain why she felt such fury, but she couldn't push it down.

His eyes hardened into blue granite. "Yeah, really. I know it's difficult, facing something that's ugly."

"Dan would never be part of anything ugly!"

Jess ignored her remark. "And I know you're scared."

"I am not scared!" she shouted. But she was. Inside, raw terror clawed at her belly.

He wheeled away from her and moved toward the open barn door. "Then c'mon out to the cornfield."

She didn't want to. She wanted to bury her head under her pillow and make it all go away—the hidden money, the Ryder gang, Jess. Mostly Jess.

Before he had tramped through her gate that day she had felt none of this growing horror. Had no doubts about Dan except that he might be dead. No confusion about an irrational attraction to a man who was not her husband.

A net was tightening around her. A net she couldn't

comprehend. She clenched her teeth until her jaw hurt. Underneath, she knew she had to move forward. Had to confront whatever was going to be.

She clumped after him in stony silence. When they reached the creek bank, Shep at her heels, Jess scooped her into his arms without asking and splashed across to set her upright at the edge of the field, where the stalks were sparse.

"When you get this far, you start crawling. Don't try to walk it, you'll be too slow. Crawl to the middle of the field, stay quiet and don't move."

"And then what?"

"I'll come for you when it's safe."

Jess watched her face as she absorbed his words. The battle within her played across her features like a goddam book. Anger. Disbelief. Fear. Bewilderment. Maybe she didn't believe one thing he'd said, but if she remembered about the cornfield, he could free his mind to lay his trap.

"Let's head back. You've got a cake to bake, remember?"

Ellen stared at him, watched the dimple slowly emerge in his tanned cheek as his smile deepened. It wasn't just a cake he wanted, she remembered. "How can you think about food at a time like this?"

"Nothing much else to do but wait. Might as well enjoy it. Besides…" He reached out to turn her toward him, and lowered his voice. "Might as well tell you, I'm thinking about more than cake."

She jerked herself free. "You are a despicable man! Conniving and deceitful and…and despicable."

He didn't answer, just moved away from her toward the creek, and after a moment, Ellen started after him. Suddenly Shep bounded away from her side and shot across the stream. In a few moments the dog's short, high-pitched barking sounded from the barnyard.

"What's wrong with Shep?" she called.

But Jess had stopped stock-still and cocked his head, listening. "It's the gate. The bell on the gate. We've got company."

Chapter Thirteen

Jess stopped on the far side of the creek, set Ellen on her feet and watched Shep streak across the ground toward the front gate. A man stepped his horse through and dismounted, his motions lazy and sure. Damn fool left the gate open, but before Jess could get up enough lather to yell at him, he recognized Dan O'Brian's distinctive, cocky walk. Gray and J.D. wouldn't be far behind.

At the thought of seeing J.D., it all came back in the flick of an eyelash, all the things Jess had tried to wipe from his memory. The filth of the prison at Richmond, the overcrowding, his escape when he knew he couldn't last another month. He remembered the agony of dragging his broken leg over back fences, through woods, across rivers. The gnawing hunger. The sharp scent of fear.

And finally the comfort he'd found in Callie's arms.

Now Jess positioned himself in front of Ellen, but kept his eyes on the Irishman, watched him jerk hard on the bridle and start for the barn. Hell, the bastard didn't spare even a glance at the house. You'd think he'd want to see his wife before he unsaddled his horse.

Shep shot across the yard and fastened his teeth on Dan's trouser leg. *Atta boy! Take a hunk out of him.*

"Get away from me," Dan growled. He tried to shake off the animal, but the snarling dog held on.

Jess smiled. *That's it, Shep. Good boy.*

Dan released the bridle. "What in the name of…" He drew back his other foot and smacked his boot into Shep's belly. "Bugger off!"

The dog yelped and slunk away to his hiding place under the back porch. Jess clenched his hands but kept quiet. Not yet. Ellen had a right to be first.

Dan swore, grabbed the bridle and again started for the barn without looking back. He hadn't changed a bit. Hated dogs more than sheriffs and loved whatever horse he was riding almost as much as he loved himself.

Ellen brushed past Jess. Instinctively he wanted to reach for her, hold her safe against him. In another minute she'd know her husband had returned. God help him, he would give anything to spare her what he knew was coming.

He stared after her for a long minute, then ducked into the shadows and began circling toward the back side of the barn. He'd stay within earshot, but he didn't want to see the reunion.

Ellen paused by the henhouse and watched a young man she did not recognize slide one dusty boot out of his stirrup and kick the gate shut. The harsh clang of the cowbell made her jerk.

"Gray, for God's sake, keep it quiet."

"What for? This here's Danny Boy's spread, ain't it?"

Ellen drew in a sharp breath, and at that moment Dan strode out of the barn. She took a step toward him. "Dan?"

"Ellie?" Her husband's tenor voice carried over the nervous clucking of her hens. "Ellie, where are you?"

She hitched her crutch tight under her arm and took another faltering step. "Dan? Is that really you?"

"Aye, honey, 'tis himself." He opened his arms. "Come to me, lass."

He wrapped his arms around her. "Sure and it's been a while, now, hasn't it?" He landed a quick, sloppy kiss on her cheek, then moved to her mouth and took his time. "Ah, Ellie honey. You sure do taste good!"

"Dan," she gasped when she could speak. "I can't believe you're here. You're home!"

"Well now," he said with a grin. "Where else d'you think I'd be?"

Ellen gave a shaky laugh. "At first I thought you might be dead, and…oh, Dan, this has been such an awful time."

"Me, dead?" He twirled one of her loose brown curls around and around his forefinger. "I'll not die so easily."

"And just last Sunday I heard you were in jail. At Riverton. It isn't true, is it? Oh, it couldn't be true!"

"Well now, lass, it is and it isn't." He grinned at her, then ostentatiously sniffed her hair. "Ah, Ellie, you smell so fine. Never met a lass who smelled as sweet as you."

Ellen flushed. "Oh, stop with your sweet-talking."

"Would you do somethin' for me, darlin'?"

"Why, of course. What is it?"

"Cook up some supper. Me and my partners are powerful hungry." He tipped his head toward the two mounted men, leaning over their saddle horns, watching Ellen with interest.

"That's Gray on the left. And J.D."

With a jaunty smile, Gray lifted his hat to reveal a mop of straw-colored curls. "Ma'am."

J.D. swept his black Stetson over his heart and bowed from the waist, but said nothing. He was dark, Ellen noted. Slicked down black hair, dark skin with a whisker shadow, eyes like slivers of coal.

"Forgive our appearance, ma'am," Gray began. "We've been riding for some while."

Dan hooted. "Ridin'! That's not just ridin', Gray. We've been hightailin' it hell-for-leather for two days straight. Sure could use a bath, honey. Don't smell good enough to come into the house."

"And some grub," Gray added.

Dan chucked Ellen under the chin. "And some grub," he echoed. "Aw, Ellie, ye look so fine."

"Well, I—" Didn't he notice her crutch?

Dan released her suddenly and turned away. "This way to the creek, boys. Let's wash up."

Gray and J.D. dismounted, tied their reins to the fence post and followed Dan across the barnyard.

Ellen watched the three men. Gray had an exuberant bounce to his step. J.D. moved his tall, elegant frame with surprising speed. And Dan, leading the way, walked the way he always did, as if he were half dancing a jig. The Pied Piper of Willow Flat.

When the back screen door flapped open, Ellen was so sure it was Dan she didn't look up from the stove.

The stew she had hastily thrown together out of leftover beans and vegetables from her garden bubbled in the big iron pot, and now she was dropping in spoonfuls of flour-and-milk mixture for dumplings. "There's coffee," she said over her shoulder. "And biscuits in the oven."

A boyish voice answered. "Thank you kindly, ma'am."

Ellen pivoted as fast as she could without tripping over her crutch. "I thought you were Dan."

The man called Gray raked off his hat. "Guess maybe you wasn't expectin' all three of us."

"No, I wasn't. I wasn't really sure about Dan until I heard about the jail—" She shut her mouth over the word.

"We ride together, Miz O'Brian. Where Danny Boy goes, J.D. and me go, too. Works t'other way as well."

"Up until the present, perhaps. Dan is home now. I don't expect he will leave again."

Gray stopped in the act of hanging his hat on a nail by the door, and gave Ellen a speculative look. "Guess he don't tell you everything, ma'am."

"I'm sure that will change, now that he is home. Sit down, Mr. Gray. My dumplings will be ready shortly."

Footsteps clunked up the back steps, along with the chink-jingle of spurs. "Gentlemen," Ellen called out. "I don't allow spurs on my kitchen floor."

Gray sank onto a chair facing the door and waited, his washed-out green eyes on the back porch. "None of us got spurs on 'cept J.D., ma'am, and I don't know as he…"

Ellen followed his gaze. With a tight feeling in her belly, she watched the slim, dark man step into the kitchen, followed by Dan. J.D. still wore his spurs.

"Perhaps you didn't hear me, gentlemen? No spurs."

Dan made a beeline for her. Putting his hands on her shoulders, he turned her back toward the stove. "Just serve up supper, Ellie," he said under his breath.

J.D. took a slow look around the room, selected the chair next to Gray and glided onto it.

"What about my floor?" Ellen muttered.

Dan nuzzled the back of her neck with his lips. "Don't fuss over it, lass. 'Tis a small thing."

She frowned at him. "Not to me it isn't. Since I'm the one who scrubs and polishes the floors around here, why shouldn't I fuss?"

Dan just grinned at her. "Ah, lass, is it dumplings I smell? Best smell on earth 'cept for your perfume."

"I don't wear perfume." She snapped out the sentence, then bit her tongue. She guessed Dan was just trying to be a good host.

He gave her another heart-melting smile, then turned to the men gathered at the table. "Boys, when you taste Ellie's dumplings you'll think you've died and gone to heaven."

"That's okay, s'long as I can git back," Gray quipped.

"This supper is as close to heaven as you're gonna get, kid." J.D.'s voice was as rough as his unshaven chin.

Ellen yanked the lid off the bubbling pot, ladled a fluffy, cream-colored dumpling into each soup bowl and smothered it with the fragrant stew.

Dan moved away from her side and sat down with a thump next to Gray. "Hell's probably a lot more fun, anyway."

"Gee, Dan, when you get there, let me know, will ya?"

J.D.'s eyes turned cold. "Both of you shut the hell up."

Ellen plunked a bowl of stew down before each man, slapped a big spoon beside it and pointedly passed out her second-best gingham napkins.

"Ellie, the coffee?" Dan suggested.

She ignored him, removed the browned biscuits from the oven and dumped them into a bowl. "Help yourself," she said crisply. "I call these my special purgatory biscuits."

J.D. snickered, but Gray looked at her with a blank expression on his young face.

"Would you gentlemen like coffee now?"

Three heads nodded and she splashed hot coffee into their mugs. For once she was glad the brew was over-boiled and bitter.

Gray slurped down a spoonful of his supper. "Mighty good stew, ma'am. Mind if I ask what all you put in it? I'm kinda partial to cookin', myself."

"Vegetables and beans," Ellen replied. "Perhaps you would like the recipe?"

Dan's eyebrows lifted. "No meat?"

"No meat. I can't afford it."

"What about the chickens?"

Ellen drew herself up to her full height and faced her husband. "My chickens lay the eggs that I sell in town to buy flour and cornmeal and coffee and everything else a farm needs to survive."

"Ah, Ellie, I didn't mean—"

"You didn't think, Dan." She reached for the empty biscuit bowl. "You never do."

Without looking up, J.D. snaked his hand out and closed it around her wrist. "I like a woman with spirit."

He tightened his fingers until her hand grew numb and she released the bowl.

"Don't hurt her, J.D.," Dan said. "She meant no harm. She's always been outspoken." He went on spooning food into his mouth.

J.D. gave her arm a sharp jerk. "I like that even better."

"Aw, come on, J.D. Let her loose. We need some more biscuits."

Ellen stared at her husband in disbelief.

A slow smile spread across J.D.'s face. "Get 'em yourself, Danny Boy. Your wife is…busy."

Ellen closed her captured hand into a fist. "Unhand me."

"In a minute," J.D. said, his voice lazy. "I like the way my fingers feel around your wrist."

Both Dan and Gray kept their gazes on the table, but a voice like cold steel came from the darkened parlor. "Take your hands off her."

Dan jerked his head up and stared into the dim room. "Who's that?"

A tall figure stepped out of the shadows and Dan's face went white. "Jess!" Dan cursed. "What are *you* doing here?"

Jess stepped into the kitchen, his Colt leveled at J.D.'s heart. "Let her go, J.D." The hammer snicked in the hushed room.

Dan's mouth gaped. "Jess, what are you doin' here? This is my house!"

"This is your wife, too. You'd think somebody needed to stand up for her."

"Well, yes. But J.D.'s only funnin', aren't ya, J.D.?"

"Sure," the man growled. But he didn't relax his hold

on Ellen's wrist. She tried to pull away, but the dark man yanked her arm again, harder.

Ellen bit back a moan and Jess thought he'd come apart. He took one step forward and jammed the gun barrel behind J.D.'s ear.

It was Callie all over again. God, he would not have survived without her help. He remembered the way it had felt when he could go on no longer—the despair, the sick feeling in the pit of his stomach. She had found him halfway across the meadow behind her father's house.

"Jason," she had said. "Jason, let me help you."

"Go back, Callie. They'll brand you a traitor, helping a Yankee. Go back before they find you with me."

"I don't care. Let me come with you."

He'd rolled away from her, let his forehead rest on the cool grass. "I can't take you with me. You belong here, in Richmond. With your family. With your Southern gentleman, Major John."

"I don't." Her long, pale face twisted. "I don't want to marry him."

"It's too late, Callie. He can't stop talking about it— your wedding next week. The whole prison is sick of hearing him." He wouldn't tell her the rest about her precious major, how he taunted the Union prisoners with promises of food, tobacco, fresh water, but never delivered. How he selected officers for special treatment in the cramped, windowless basement room. He could still hear the screams at night. He could still feel the steel chain they'd used on him.

"Jason, please. Listen to me. John is… I am afraid of him sometimes."

Oh, God, not Callie. She'd come to the prison every day, bringing food, bandages, soap. Without her and the other Southern women who braved the surly Confederate guards to help hundreds of enemy prisoners, they all would have died. He owed her his life.

"Has he hurt you?"

She didn't answer for a long time. "You must take me with you."

Jess groaned. "He'll know. He'll kill us both."

She was silent, her slim white hands clenching her skirt. Finally she touched his stubbled cheek. "He will kill me anyway, Jason. I know it as surely as I know my father is unaware of the abuses at the prison."

"You have to tell him, Callie. It has to stop. Men are dying."

"I know. Yes, I will tell him. Tonight. And then I will have my carriage brought around as if I were going…going to a ladies' prayer meeting. I will meet you at the end of the lane at midnight."

He had had no choice. Callie was not safe, would never be safe with Major John D. Stedman. Jess wasn't sorry for what he'd done. He was sorry only for what had followed.

Now, in the kitchen at Ellen's ranch, J.D. didn't move a muscle. "Just out of curiosity, Flint, what business is this of yours?"

"Yeah, Jess," Dan echoed. "Where do you come into this?"

"I came for my share of the money. Then—"

Ellen interrupted. "I fell in the creek and broke my leg. Mr. Flint has been helping me with the chores."

J.D. released her wrist. Jess saw the marks where his fingers had bitten into her skin, and for the first time in his life he knew what it would feel like to kill someone in cold blood.

J.D. curled his lip in a sneer. "Now, that's real touching, isn't it, boys? I just wonder how she paid him?"

Before Jess could react, Ellen whirled and slapped J.D.'s face so hard the crack of her palm against his skin sounded like a pistol shot.

Dan half rose from the table. "You're outta line, Ellie."

"No," she said, her voice oddly quiet. "I am not."

J.D. lifted his spoon and calmly resumed eating, as if nothing unusual had occurred. "Sit down, Danny Boy."

Dan sank back onto his chair.

Jess struggled to control his rage. At that moment he wanted to pistol-whip the Irishman until he couldn't flash that baby-faced grin ever again. He glanced across the room and caught Ellen's gaze. Her eyes were dilated, her cheeks flushed. But her mouth was compressed into a thin, determined line.

"Mr. Flint?" she said in a low, steady voice.

Jess nodded his head. "Yes, Mrs. O'Brian?"

Ellen turned her gaze to study her husband, then she perused Gray, then J.D., and then Dan once more, a thoughtful look on her white face.

"Mr. Flint." She pointedly addressed him. "I am ready to retire. Would you assist me up the stairs?"

Chapter Fourteen

Dan shot a narrow-eyed look at Jess. "You watch yourself, boyo."

"Always do," Jess replied in a level tone. That brought a snort of derision from J.D., but Jess ignored him.

"Just the same," Dan continued, his mouth half-full of biscuit, "she's mine. Remember that."

"I don't need you to remind me that Mrs. O'Brian is a married woman."

J.D. flexed his fingers and grasped his coffee mug. "That's a surprise," he muttered. "Gettin' old, Jess?"

"Nope. Just careful."

J.D.'s voice turned silky. "I'd watch my back if I were you."

Dan swallowed his mouthful of food. "Ellie, honey? I'll be along in a while. Gotta finish my supper and show the boys where to bed down for the night."

Ellen looked at her husband without answering, an expression in her blue eyes Jess had never seen before. She looked as if she'd been walloped in the belly by a bale of hay. Gently he turned her toward the parlor. "Come on. I'll help you up the stairs."

Without a word, she limped on through the doorway and paused at the bottom of the staircase. Jess settled his hands at her waist and lifted her, one laborious step at a time, until they reached the landing. At the door to her bedroom, he stopped her with a hand on her shoulder.

"Are you all right?"

Ellen gave an unladylike snort and twisted toward him. Her eyes looked as if they'd shoot daggers at any moment, and her mouth—her mouth was pursed into a tight little O like a dried-up rosebud.

"At the moment, I am cross as a bear."

"About?"

"I should think that is obvious. First of all, my husband, it appears, has the spine of a green onion. Then there's the matter of my kitchen floor, which is getting spur-marked as we speak. And then..." She stopped, tears glittering in her eyes.

Jess fought the urge to pull her into his arms. "That's plenty for a good lather, I guess."

"And then," she said with venom in her voice, "there's *you.*"

"Me? Hell, lady, I'm on your side. I'm the only friend you've got in this upside-down situation."

"Jess, I have to be frank. I don't know who to trust. I am so tired and rattled inside I don't know what I think or feel anymore." With a soft moan she added, "This isn't what I expected. And none of it makes any sense!"

"Yeah, it does, Ellen. If you've got the sand to look at it head-on."